TO HELL AND BACK

TO HELL AND BACK

TRIALS AND TRIBULATIONS BOOK 3

NATALIE GREY
MICHAEL ANDERLE

DISRUPTIVE IMAGINATION

To Family, Friends and
Those Who Love
to Read.
May We All Enjoy Grace
to Live the Life We Are
Called.

PROLOGUE

Gordes, France

Emeric Carre strode along the corridor to the administrator's office.

The view out the windows showed nothing but greenery. The facility near Gordes was hidden in the trees, practically invisible until you were right on top of it.

That was what his scouts reported, anyway. He'd sent them to determine the distance to the nearest town and find out anything they could—with strict instructions that they were not to harm any of the townspeople.

Yet.

Someday soon, many people would find out that ignorance was not a valid excuse for letting thousands be enslaved and tortured. They were going to find out how powerful revenge could be.

He opened the door to the office and glanced around the room as he entered. There was at least one of his Wechselbalg at every computer terminal, some murmuring to one another as they worked their way through the computer systems.

They hadn't found the other facilities yet, but they knew those facilities existed.

And when they found them, Emeric would have his army.

He did not know what had happened to Hugo Marcari, and he did not much care. He assumed it had been a power struggle of some sort. The man who had come to their facility—his security pass said Gerard Cordova—must have been trying to take control.

They had killed Gerard for his part in it. Emeric smiled. The look of fear in the man's eyes was something he remembered fondly. Gerard, like all the scientists here, had known exactly what he was doing. He had deserved to die.

As did the rest of them—the people who had sold these buildings to Hugo Marcari, the government officials who had taken bribes and turned a blind eye, the villagers who had heard gunfire and screams and done nothing.

The world would learn the cost. It had allowed Hugo Marcari to build an army, and now that Hugo was gone, that army had a mind of its own.

Emeric growled softly. He was itching to transform and run into the village. He wanted to begin taking his revenge now.

He had to wait, though. He had to be patient.

He had to find those other facilities and free his brethren.

"I think I have the list!" someone called.

Emeric smiled. At last. *At last.*

QBS *ArchAngel*

Stephen laughed as he and Bethany Anne made their way through the corridors of the *ArchAngel*, "You're really going to go deal with a couple of mobsters?"

After the past few days, it felt good to laugh—especially since he was on tenterhooks waiting for his team to be released for combat again so they could clear out the remaining facilities. Bethany Anne was providing a much-needed distraction.

He had been informed yesterday that she was planning to go deal with a new underworld that was emerging in the vacuum *he* had evidently created when he took out some of their leaders a few years back.

It had been part of his atonement; cleaning up the messes that had flourished when he had withdrawn from the world in defeat. Until now, he thought he had been successful. They all had.

But apparently, the low-level scum who'd taken over

were taking jobs from humans, assassinating outsiders, and exposing the Unknown World to public scrutiny when that was absolutely the last thing Bethany Anne needed.

Still. A couple of chumps too low level to have gotten taken out last time? Bethany Anne's talents really were wasted on that.

"I am going out of my mind in here." Bethany Anne shook her head. "After the clusterfuck, you went through with Hugo, I am in no mood to take shit. If they want to test me? I'm gonna show them what happens."

"Well, you can always come with us to take Gerard down." Stephen smiled at her. "Don't tell me you haven't dreamed of getting a few shots in on him."

"Oh, I have," Bethany Anne assured him. "But I'd never dream of taking Hsu and Jennifer's revenge away from them." She grinned. "Any luck figuring out where he is?"

"ADAM's working on it," Stephen explained. "He hasn't shown up yet at any of the facilities on our list, which I can only assume means that he knows 'Hugo' sent a message condemning him."

One of Stephen's last acts at Hugo's hideout—before, of course, erasing any trace of Wechselbalg activity that human detectives might stumble across—had been to send a message to all research facilities, saying that Gerard was a criminal and should not be trusted.

He'd also told them to begin shutting down research, and that his deputies would be there shortly to evacuate the scientists and transport the Wechselbalg.

Those scientists were in for a surprise. They weren't going to be searching for any new jobs after this. They were going to be judged by the Queen's representative.

Stephen didn't think much for their chances.

"What are you going to do first?" Bethany Anne asked him. She pushed open the door to her temporary rooms on the *ArchAngel* and smiled as Ashur looked up from his dog bed with a giant yawn.

"Hello again, Ashur," Stephen said politely.

Bethany Anne laughed. "Why are you so stuffy?"

"Ashur and I are both gentlemen. I think he appreciates that I treat him as such."

Ashur chuffed and pushed himself up to nose at Stephen's hand.

"See?" Stephen asked Bethany Anne.

"Yes, yes." She took a seat and grinned at him, running her hands through Ashur's fur while the dog wagged happily. "So, what are your plans?"

"Well, the plan *was* to track Gerard, but since he hasn't turned up anywhere, I'm going to go get the facilities resolved."

Stephen dropped into a chair and tried not to tip his head back with a groan. Manners dictated that he sit straight, but he was exhausted. He'd bought himself a few hours of rest with his directive to shut the experiments down, but he didn't want to leave the rescue any longer than that.

All he could think of was Jennifer shut up in those facilities. And she'd been a scientist. What if she'd been a captive?

He winced involuntarily.

Bethany Anne asked quietly. "Are you all right?"

Stephen nodded jerkily. "Yes. I just want to finish this… now. I want to get them out of there."

"At least rest for a few minutes," Bethany Anne advised him. "You may not get tired the way you used to, but there's only so long you can fixate on one thing before your mind gets worn out."

"I know. I know. I just keep thinking of the Wechselbalg still in their cages and—"

"I know," she told him gently. "But you came back here, and the first thing you did was make a plan to make sure Gerard couldn't hurt anybody else. You're ready to kill him as soon as he pops up. You've already picked a strike team for each facility. It's only been ten hours, Stephen, and the experiments have stopped—ADAM has confirmed that. You're doing everything you can." She smiled and patted his knee. "Tell you what—go find Jennifer. Have a romantic dinner."

"We just had a romantic dinner. Also, it's...six in the morning."

"Do *something* to take your mind off this. It's only going to be a few more hours until Sergio, Hsu, and the rest are fully healed. ADAM is forging security passes. This will all go smoother and have less chance of failure if you take the time you need to prepare."

"Why do you always have to be sensible?" Stephen asked with a grin. "Thanks for the reminder. And good luck with the mobsters, by the way."

"You make it sound like they're from the twenties."

"I liked the twenties. They had style." Stephen smiled at her. "When are you leaving?"

"In a few minutes. You're sure you don't need Pete?"

"Nah. A lot of the people from the Velingrad facility are

going to help." Stephen tipped an imaginary hat to her. "Good hunting, my Queen."

"Good hunting, Stephen."

"There you are." Arisha hurried across the wide recreational deck and joined Jennifer at a window.

She immediately wished she hadn't. Earth was mesmerizing, glowing white and blue and green below them, but it was also very, very far down.

And space was about six inches away from her.

Even after being on the *Meredith Reynolds,* she still wasn't used to this. Arisha gave a little whimper at the void outside and looked away.

"Don't like space?" Jennifer said sympathetically.

"I would think you of all people would understand!" Arisha shuddered. "Didn't you say you missed Earth?"

Jennifer laughed. "Sure. And I do! But this view...there's nothing like it."

"Agreed. Humans were never meant to see such things."

Jennifer laughed again. "Oh, come on. Look. I promise you're perfectly safe."

Arisha opened one eye and gave a look out into the black before squeaking in terror and squeezing both eyes shut.

"Now, now," Jennifer said. "Come on, you can do this."

"All right." Arisha hunched her shoulders and looked. "I'm looking."

"Look how beautiful it is," Jennifer said quietly. "That's

our home. That's where our parents were born, where almost everyone we love lives."

Arisha felt herself relax slightly, "I guess that's true."

"Yeah," Jennifer said encouragingly. "You can see the mountains like little ripples on the surface. You can see the clouds and their shadows. Isn't that amazing? Seeing the whole world like this, it makes you realize what's really important."

Arisha looked at her wordlessly.

Jennifer hesitated. "When I was in the facility in Spain," she explained quietly. "I realized that the only thing that mattered was whether I could live with myself. If, when I went to bed each night, I believed that I'd done everything in my power to make the world the best place it could be for the people I love. And I understand now that if I leave TQB and go home…I will always know that I didn't do my best. I didn't do everything I could. If I leave, I'll always know that I left the people I loved to fight without me. I can't do that and live with myself."

Arisha found herself smiling. Jennifer looked more content now than she had before, more at ease in her own skin. "So, you think…"

"I think I'm going to tell them that it doesn't matter about the five years. I'm here for good." Jennifer smiled at her.

She truly was happier now that she had made this decision. She could not remember being so content in the past few years. Her love for Stephen had seemed like one more thing pulling her away from her home—something she could not give up, and yet also something that she could not help but fear, in a way. It would change her life in ways she couldn't know yet.

Now, she understood it as a part of her. She loved this planet, and she would protect it.

She crossed her arms, leaned against the window, and laughed when Arisha yelped.

"I'm perfectly safe. What about you, huh? You think you'll stick around?" She poked Arisha in the arm. "I hear Stoyan is trying to decide, too."

Arisha blushed bright red. "I...I don't know what you're talking about," she spluttered.

"You think you two could settle down on an asteroid?" Jennifer asked wickedly. "Raise kids, have a happy little home?"

Arisha covered her face with her hands. "Stop it! I haven't thought about any of that yet! I just..."

"Light up every time you think about him?" Jennifer said mischievously. She saw Stephen appear across the room and smiled at him.

"You do it, too," Arisha pointed out. She nodded at Stephen.

"Oh, I know." Jennifer smiled. She waited as Stephen crossed the room. "What's going on?"

"Nothing. Just waiting to start the last part of this mission." Stephen shook his head. "I'm not feeling very patient."

"Well, don't tell Sergio that," Arisha advised. "He's not quite healed, but he's already talking about running off and saving people. If you encourage him, he will re-injure himself."

Stephen nodded. "I know. How is he doing?"

"Physically, he should be back to normal in a few hours," Jennifer explained. "Most of what was done to him was superficial enough to heal quickly even without our intervention. However, it will take him some time to come to terms with what happened."

"Well, you know what they say about that," Stephen said. "Nothing heals better than bringing justice to the people who hurt you."

"You have weird sayings in Romania," Jennifer informed him with a grin. She looped her arm through his and kissed him on the cheek. "But very handsome men."

"Oh, I don't know. Not as handsome as Bulgarian men, I hear." Stephen gave Arisha a teasing grin. "How *is* Stoyan doing, by the way?"

"I hate you both," Arisha announced. She marched away with her nose in the air.

"Give him our regards," Stephen called.

***

ECCENTRIC BILLIONAIRE FOUND DEAD, the headlines screamed.

ADAM perused the article, lingering on colloquialisms in the text. The more he learned about humans, the more intriguing he found language and translation. It still baffled him that there was no universally accepted way to describe phenomena.

Humans were so strange.

Hugo Marcari, the sole heir to the once-prominent Marcari family, was found dead early this morning in his family castle along with the entirety of his staff, after a gruesome accident.

Speaking about the grisly scene, Police Commissioner Gomez-Alvarez said, "It appears that Mr. Marcari had grown paranoid, and installed many security systems and booby traps to protect himself from intruders. Unfortunately, it seems that these devices were triggered accidentally and killed Mr. Marcari and his staff.

"In light of this tragedy, we would like to remind the community that these devices are very dangerous and can impede rescue efforts if you should ever find yourself in this type of dangerous situation."

It is unknown at this stage whether any of the inhabitants of the castle accidentally or purposefully triggered the mechanisms, but the commissioner stated that, though efforts to inspect the castle were being impeded by fears of further traps, there were no signs of foul play at this stage.

In the nearby town, reactions to the deaths ranged widely.

"I always knew there was something wrong with that one," Maria Quintana, a longtime inhabitant of the town, said. "Never saw him in town, you didn't, and he was always bringing in outsiders to work at the castle. I'm not at all surprised."

However, Ricardo Bover, who moved back to the town recently after working in Madrid, expressed concern for the families of the castle staff. "I only hope that the estate has enough money to help out those poor families," she said. "It's a terrible tragedy."

ADAM was amused by this. Stephen had laid the groundwork to get the bodies of the hired guards out of the castle and place the bodies of the servants next to the defense mechanisms, which would have produced somewhat similar marks to the Wechselbalg claws and teeth.

He wondered if he would feel sympathy for the castle staff if he were human.

He pondered it and decided that he would not. Stephen and Jennifer, who swept the castle, had explained the staff was aware of what happened at the facility and that none had brought the matter to the authorities.

As Stephen said, they had been judged.

One of the guards, a man named Adolfo, had tried to report Hugo to the authorities. Unfortunately, due to Hugo's bribes, the authorities had not passed along his concerns—and had given his name to Hugo. Adolfo's body had been found in the laboratories.

As ADAM was considering this, one of his sub processes hit pay dirt. Intrigued, he brought up the satellite imagery.

It was the helicopter Gerard had taken from Spain.

Finally. ADAM tracked the helicopter, but it had gone silent and seemed to be equipped with some sort of camouflage within the rotors to render it invisible on satellite imagery. ADAM had developed a program to outsmart that piece of technology if he found the helicopter again, but so far, nothing.

In the meantime, he had been searching for distinctive fragments of the code Hugo used to restrict communications at the facilities, and he had found a location match that was not one of the facilities Tabitha had identified. It was in France, near a small town called Gordes.

And there, on the roof, was the helicopter.

"Stephen?"

"Yes, ADAM?" Stephen's eagerness to begin the mission was palpable.

"I found Gerard's helicopter," ADAM informed him. "It is at a site that may be a research facility, though it is not one that Tabitha found. It is possible only Hugo and Gerard knew this location."

Stephen swore under his breath. *Trust those bastards to have something else up their sleeves. When we find Gerard, I am bringing Barnabas with me so I can make sure there is nothing else he is hiding. Otherwise, I will always wonder about additional unknown facilities.*

"I have devised many ideas to ensure we find all facilities," ADAM assured him. "One of them provided the location of the helicopter. I will tell you more at a more opportune time. For now, I assume the mechanics do not interest you."

"I will be in the conference room in a moment with the team. Find everything pertinent to that place that you can and get a Pod ready."

"I will do so immediately."

2

QBS *ArchAngel*

Ten minutes later, Stephen, Jennifer, and Irina were clustered around printouts of the satellite images, along with a few grainy images that seemed to show Gerard's arrival late the day before.

Jennifer's lips moved silently as she traced the distance on a nearby map.

"He would have arrived with just enough time to fly from Spain, with one stop for fuel."

Stephen looked at her. He knew her mind was hard at work on the problem, and she was coming to a conclusion.

"He had a plan in place," Jennifer said finally. "He left without confirmation that Hugo was dead. Either he knew some other way, or he was prepared for a power struggle."

Irina nodded. "I wouldn't be surprised if it was the second one."

Though she had observed Gerard briefly, mostly hearing snatches of conversation between the scientists instead, she had known that Gerard was dangerous—in many ways, more dangerous than Hugo.

She had always wondered what would happen if he decided to break with his employer.

It appeared they were finding out.

Stephen shook his head. "He left Hugo to die. That's all it is. He's a coward."

"He saw us storm the other facilities," Jennifer observed dryly. "He probably knew there was no chance of getting to the castle in time. He would have been too late, judging by when he left."

"I don't care." Stephen looked grim. "He was loyal to Hugo, he did everything in Hugo's name—then when the danger came, he abandoned the man he was paid to protect. That speaks of a coward. Cowards like to hide behind the odds."

Jennifer nodded, but a smile broke across her face a second later. "Of course, Hugo never had the knack of getting loyalty in the first place. There's a reason he ended up with spineless bullies."

"That, I'll give you." Stephen blew out his breath. "ADAM, do you think—"

The door opened, and Arisha slipped in with Stoyan. Both of them had mussed hair, and Stoyan's shirt was buttoned incorrectly.

The corners of Irina's mouth twitched.

"You said you needed us?" Stoyan was clearly trying to sound nonchalant.

Stephen, thinking back on his centuries of hurried trysts in noble's gardens, and passionate affairs with courtesans across Europe, forbore to comment. "Yes. We've found Gerard."

"Gerard." Arisha went to the table at once, seizing the images. "Hsu's going to want to see this, too, I suppose."

"But you want the chance to kill him first?" Irina suggested. She smiled at Arisha.

"The man's a psychopath," Arisha said flatly. Unconsciously, her hand went to her shoulder. As a human, she did not have the fast-healing capabilities of the Wechselbalg, and she still carried the marks Gerard gave her as he tried to kill her in Spain.

Stoyan growled slightly when he saw the bruises. "I wouldn't mind a shot at that man, myself."

"Whoever sees him, kills him," Stephen said warningly. "No waiting, no letting everyone get a shot in. Arisha's right—he's dangerous, but he's also slippery. Don't let him get away."

He looked around the room and met each person's eyes, waiting until they nodded.

"Good. Now that's settled—ADAM, do you know if the facility in France received my message about Gerard?"

"It's difficult to say." ADAM's voice came over the speakers of the conference room. "I sent it via a channel that broadcast to all scientific research facilities. In that case, it might have transmitted to this one—if it is, in fact, a research facility. However, although I was able to get into some of the facilities, I have not yet been able to establish a link to this one. Hugo wanted to make sure it would be very difficult to find his entire operation...and unfortunately, he was good at hiding it."

Stephen considered this. "Do you think you could get a message to them now?" he asked ADAM.

"Yes. There is a dish on the roof. I could send a message."

"Send them a message reiterating the danger that Gerard poses," Stephen said finally. "And tell them again that per Hugo's instructions, the experiments are to be ended."

His mind turned over the different possibilities. There was a chance that if Gerard were cornered, he would lash out. But Stephen had no desire to storm another facility unless it was truly necessary. If he could get the staff of this facility to turn against Gerard, there was the chance that they would allow them in without a fight.

He looked at Jennifer. "Do we warn them that we're coming?"

"We're going now?" He saw the relief on her face. "Good. I don't think I could wait another minute. And...I don't know. If they knew they only had to detain him for a few minutes, they might try harder. But I don't want him to escape."

The rest of the group nodded.

"ADAM, tell them we are coming to pick up Gerard," Stephen decided. "I don't want them to put up a fight, and I want them to know that Gerard cannot be allowed to escape."

"I will do so."

"All right." Stephen looked around the room. "Get ready. We're going now. We'll wait for the others to recover before we go after the other facilities, but we don't have time on this one."

Gordes, France

"Sir?" One of the Wechselbalg, a woman, named Marie with a heart-shaped face and hazel eyes, beckoned Emeric over to the desk. "We have an incoming message that appears to be from Hugo."

"Another one?" Emeric shook his head. "I don't want to hear it."

"Sir, it's important." She looked worried. "They say they're coming here. *Now.*"

"*What?*" Emeric was at her side in a moment, scanning the message.

GERARD CORDOVA IS ACTING WITHOUT ORDERS FROM HUGO MARCARI, the message read. *HE IS TO BE APPREHENDED SO THAT HE MAY FACE JUSTICE. THE EXPERIMENTATION PROGRAM SHOULD CEASE IMMEDIATELY. ALL STAFF WILL BE PROVIDED WITH ESCORT FROM THE PREMISES, AND PERSONNEL WILL MAKE SURE ALL EXPERIMENTS ARE EVACUATED SAFELY. WE WILL ARRIVE SOON.*

"What does 'soon' mean?" Emeric asked furiously. He slammed his hand down onto the back of Marie's chair. He was fuming.

They needed more time to learn everything they could of the program and its participants.

"Would you like me to send a message back, sir?" Marie was gazing up at him.

"No! No. Everyone, get ready to run. We're leaving now."

They would just have to get their information at the next facility.

"What do we do about the bodies, sir?" one of the Wechselbalg asked.

Emeric looked around at all of them and, despite their odds, felt his chest swell with pride. These were the strong ones, the ones who had not only survived their torture but endured it long enough to pick their moment and strike out in revenge.

And they had all sensed the opportunity in the same moment.

When the message had come to stop the experiments, the scientists had been confused...and they had made mistakes. Cages had been left ajar, and Wechselbalg had been left in the experiment rooms without restraints.

For most of those scientists, that was the last thing they ever did.

A moment of distraction was all it took to lose your badge—or the keys to a cage. A moment of distraction was all it took to turn your back on an unchained Wechselbalg who now had no orders.

A moment of distraction was all it took to wind up dead.

Emeric wouldn't make the same mistake. If Hugo was sending more guards and personnel, they could have weapons that would hurt his new pack.

Emeric must protect them. And he did not intend to die here before he got his revenge.

"Burn the bodies," he ordered. "Pile them in the court-yard—naked."

They stared at him silently, not understanding.

"If they know we killed the scientists and escaped, they're going to hunt us down," Emeric explained. "But if they think that pile of bodies means the scientists killed us and fled, they'll probably let them go."

"Move quickly. As soon as we're done, we need to get into the forest and hide." He paused. "And I want three volunteers. I want to see these people Hugo has sent. We may see them again."

———

Jennifer packed the last of her Wechselbalg armor into a small bag and swung it onto her back. Nearby, Stephen prepared silently, strapping armor on over his bare skin and pulling a black shirt on over it.

"Hey," Jennifer called softly.

He looked up at her wordlessly, and she saw the pain in his eyes.

"Listen." Jennifer went over to him and took one of his hands in both of hers. "You aren't Wechselbalg. If you were, you would have been raised on the stories of mad scientists who wanted to harness our power."

Stephen stared at her silently.

"I guess what I mean is..." She paused and sighed before continuing. "Hold yourself accountable for things you do wrong, sure. It's one of the things I like about you. You don't make excuses. But sometimes you take responsibility for things that were never your fault. There will always be someone like Hugo. Nothing you do can prevent that."

"I know, but—"

"No. You don't." Jennifer gave him a rueful smile. "And

it's going to drive you crazy if you keep thinking that way." She grinned impishly. "Plus, it'll give you frown lines."

Stephen laughed. "I am so lucky I have you. You know, there aren't many other people who would talk to me that way."

"Exactly. That's why you're right—you are lucky you have me." Jennifer checked her magazines and gave him a smile. "Let's go kick some ass."

3

QBS *ArchAngel*

The sound of bubbling filled the room as Bobcat wove between tanks of beer and made his way to the back.

He was taking an awful risk with this.

There was a set of tanks in his office right now, supposedly brewing the beer he would use in the competition between himself, Marcus, and William.

However, the real competition beer was here, in with the tanks that held the beer for the bar. He'd set it all up at three in the morning one time when the station was fast asleep.

He wouldn't be able to test it for a month, but he could practically taste it: perfectly balanced, malt and hops blending into a symphony of taste that would sweep across—

"Bobcat. You in here?"

Bobcat pulled his head up from where he had been

leaning lovingly against the tank, running his hand over the smooth vat.

He cleared his throat. "Yeah, what's up?"

John stooped as he carefully made his way through the room. The warrior looked around himself, nodding happily.

"This is awesome. Never been in here before."

"Yeah." Bobcat tried to look nonchalant, but his mind was racing. Was John a spy for one of the others? Was he trying to sabotage the beer?

"Everything okay?" John frowned at him.

"Oh, yeah. Just didn't…sleep…well. What can I do for you?" Bobcat clapped the other man on the shoulder and led him away from the tank.

"I'll be going with Bethany Anne to check out a few wannabe big shots in the underworld—Wechselbalg taking hit jobs from humans."

Bobcat gave a low whistle. There had always been some overlap between the fringes of the Unknown World and the human underworld, but such overlap was strictly forbidden. Letting humans know about the shifters that walked in their midst would open a can of worms no one wanted.

Of course, some people—Wechselbalg who had been thrown out of their packs, for instance, and who were scraping out a bare existence in the cities—tended not to care much. They'd gladly watch their brethren burn just for revenge.

"I thought Bethany Anne had been trying not to get involved in that stuff, though," Bobcat clarified.

"She was. But I think this thing with Hugo may have

gotten her a bit...angry." John grinned. "I have to say, I'm looking forward to watching those guys get the ass-kicking they deserve."

The two men emerged into the brightness of the bar, Bobcat wiping his hands on a towel.

"Anyway," John explained, "she wants to bring Ashur with us, and thought maybe you could give us some ideas on a camouflaged shelter for him—something like the camo pattern on some of your birds."

"Yeah, I could totally do that," Bobcat agreed. "Actually, I think I have some of the material laying around. How soon were you going to leave?"

"Well...they're going pretty much now, I was just going to stay and get the shelter and go later with Ashur. But if we can do this pretty quickly, all the better."

"No problem at all. Come on, we'll go dig that stuff up now and get it adhered."

Conscious of William at the bar, Bobcat did not want to betray himself by looking over his shoulder toward the brewing room. But he made a promise to the beer:

I'll be back.

"What are we waiting for?" Pete asked the others.

Eric, doing a last minute check on one of his weapons, gave a shrug. "No idea, man."

Ecaterina, running her fingers through Ashur's white fur, also shrugged. She seemed content to wait on the floor of Bethany Anne's rooms, leaning up against Ashur's side.

Ashur, for his part, was perfectly content to sit still

anywhere provided he was being adored. He grinned, tongue lolling out of his mouth as Ecaterina rubbed his tummy.

"You're such a stone-cold killer," Pete told him.

Ashur chuffed and looked away.

The doors slid open, and Bethany Anne and John walked in. John carried a folded contraption, each side was coated in a white, pale brown, and black camouflage.

Pete nodded his head at it, "What's that?"

"*This* is going to be a little hideaway for Ashur," John explained. He held it out as Ashur heaved himself up and came over to sniff the box. The dog gave John a dubious look. "You're going to like it," John assured him. "And you'll be all camouflaged. You'll get to chase rabbits all night instead of being cooped up in a hotel room."

Ashur gave a happy chuff and sat down next to Bethany Anne, his tongue lolling out of his mouth.

"I don't suppose you could get me a tent so I could camp, too," Ecaterina said wistfully.

"It's going to be *cold*," Bethany Anne reminded her. "And I promised your husband that I would take care of you."

"And I promised my husband that if he went around making people promise that, he and I were going to have *words*," Ecaterina said matter-of-factly. "Winter camping is fun. It reminds me of going out on my own, away from everything." She smiled nostalgically.

"Winter camping…like, in the snow?" Eric asked, incredulous.

Ecaterina rolled her eyes, "Yeah, like in the snow. Come on, Ashur, you and I know how it is."

Ashur smiled at her.

"Everyone ready?" Bethany Anne asked them all. They nodded, and she gave a grim smile. "Right. Let's go show some stupid assassins that breaking my rules can be dangerous for your health."

Gordes, France

The Pod touched down in the woods, a little ways from the facility. The door slid open with a hiss, and Stephen climbed out, reaching back to offer Jennifer his hand as she stepped down.

She grinned at him. The unconscious mannerisms of his past were adorable to her. No one had ever treated her that way before. The other Wechselbalg in Denver wanted to treat her either as a helpless woman who enjoyed soft, feminine things or as a warrior with no other facets to her personality.

She liked that Stephen seemed to realize she could be both.

"It's quiet," Stephen murmured to her, his voice far too low for an ordinary human to catch.

Jennifer nodded as they moved silently through the underbrush.

"There are no animals. I'll bet what they did in this facility scared everything off."

"You think so?" Stephen asked her, surprised.

"Definitely. Animals are way smarter than humans that way. They see something dangerous, smell poison or hear screams, and they head the other way. Humans want to go look and see what's up—they don't trust their instincts."

"Maybe they want to help the people that are trapped in there," Stephen pointed out. "Like us."

"That's an awful lot of credit to give most humans." Jennifer snickered softly.

They both drew into the shadows as they reached the edge of the trees.

The facility was surrounded by about fifty yards of cleared ground on each side, with high fences edged in barbed wire. Floodlights swept over the grass in what seemed to be random patterns.

Stephen looked at Jennifer, assessing her profile as she looked at the facility. This place was a prison, and while a paltry distance of fifty yards and a fence—even with barbed wire—would never stop a healthy Wechselbalg, it might well keep in one who was malnourished, beaten, and being tortured by the command waves used to give orders.

"How do they justify it to themselves?" she asked quietly.

"They won't for much longer." It was the best he could give her. "They're going to see Gerard get what he deserves, and then they'll be judged, too."

They made their way around to the main gate, careful to stay within the shadow of the trees, and put on the last pieces of their uniforms—a suit jacket for Stephen and a lab coat for Jennifer. The backpack that held Jennifer's Wechselbalg armor converted to a stylish handbag, and Stephen tugged slightly on his suit jacket to keep the outline of the pistols from showing.

They swiped the counterfeit badges ADAM had created, and the gates began to shudder open.

"How long do you think it will take before someone

tries to stop us?" Jennifer asked. "I can't decide if I think they'll want us to save them from Gerard...or if they'll be trying to attack us at his command."

"Maybe a little of both," Stephen suggested.

They walked up the gravel driveway to the main door, surrounded by silence.

"Something is wrong," Stephen said quietly.

"I'll second that." Jennifer looked around herself. "But what? Lights are on, the building's running."

"No patrols," Stephen pointed out. "Haven't seen anyone in the windows, either."

Jennifer gave him a worried look and swiped her badge at the main door. The lights flickered green, and she pulled the door open, half-cringing as she waited for an alarm. Alarms *hurt* when you had an especially good sense of hearing.

But no alarms sounded.

They walked down a long hallway lit by fluorescent bulbs, lined with age-stained but otherwise-clean linoleum. Whatever had happened, it hadn't left scorch marks and bloodstains, the way it had at the other facilities.

But there was still empty silence.

Then they got to the second floor.

Jennifer pressed a hand over her mouth with a little cry. Blood spattered the walls and streaked along the floor. She started running, stopping in each laboratory, but the cages were empty, and there was blood in every room.

They ran up the stairs, through the rest of the laboratories, and kicked down the doors to the conference rooms.

Nothing. No one.

"**Stephen, people are loading into vehicles on the far side of the building, and the helicopter engine just started.**"

"Get to the roof!" Stephen took off, streaking down the corridor. "ADAM, do whatever the hell you have to. An Act of *God* if you have to, call down a storm, I don't care, keep that helicopter from lifting off!"

"I will do what I can." ADAM, having learned something about tone of voice, did not point out that he was not able to call down storms or acts of God. "I am attempting to scramble their guidance and communications, which may keep them from lifting off while they troubleshoot."

"You're a genius, ADAM." Stephen managed a grin.

Jennifer pulled into the lead, her eyes narrowed. She yanked off her lab coat, careless of the buttons, so she could have free access to the two pistols, and burst out onto the roof with a yell, guns pointed at the chopper.

At the empty chopper.

Jennifer and Stephen stared at one another, chests heaving.

"The trucks! Go!" Jennifer yelled.

They ran to the edge of the roof and—with a brief check for guns and debris below—jumped.

"The fire!" Stephen yelled behind her. A bonfire blazed off to one side.

"I saw it!" Jennifer landed with a gasp and a thud and rolled on the gravel. The trucks were already gone into the night...

Beside them, in a flaming heap, were bodies. Dozens of bodies.

They froze. Jennifer looked as if she were about to lose her lunch all over the gravel.

Then, to Stephen's shock, she leaned forward and sniffed delicately. A curious look came over her face.

"What is it?" Stephen asked her.

"I don't think any of these are Wechselbalg." Jennifer looked at the pile of bodies, then back to Stephen. "I think these are the guards and the scientists."

Stephen jerked his head back to the pile. "Do you think Gerard is in here?"

"That'd be some good luck for a change," Jennifer muttered. "ADAM? Any way we could find out?"

"I'm afraid I don't have very good news," ADAM reported. "A message was just sent to all scientific facilities, saying that Gerard will be arriving shortly to collect the 'experiments.' It says that any further communications from Hugo are not to be trusted."

"So if those aren't the experiments...and all the guards are dead..." Stephen frowned. "Were there any commands executed before we got into the facility, ADAM? Can you tell?"

"Unfortunately, I can't. I can offer no conjecture, only the same facts you have observed: somehow, Gerard is still alive, and he has the Wechselbalg with him."

"Maybe he's a captive," Stephen suggested.

"Maybe." Jennifer gave him a look. "And maybe he's fed them some lie that he's the one saving them from all this, instead of the truth that he was Hugo's right-hand man. And if they believe him? They're going to fight us to keep him safe."

Stephen took a deep breath to steady himself.

"We have to evacuate those other facilities," Jennifer told him. "Right now. Before he has the chance to grow his army. Then we can worry about the people who are loyal to him."

"Good idea. *ArchAngel*, standby—we'll be back to the Pod in a few minutes. And tell anyone who's back on their feet to get ready for a ground assault. We're clearing those facilities out tonight."

4

QBS *ArchAngel*

Hsu winced as she pulled on slacks, a blouse, and a lab coat. Her shoulder was mostly healed, much to her surprise. She'd become used to the ridiculously fast healing abilities of the Wechselbalg, but this was even beyond that.

The doctors on board had worked some magic in the medical lab.

She brushed her hair out of her eyes and frowned in surprise at herself in the mirror. Really, she was looking better than she had in years. Her face was smoother, and she had less grey in her hair.

That *had* to be her imagination, right?

She looked at her shoulder again and bit her lip. She was fine. She was here. But back in the stairwell of the labs, back on the roof as Stephen leaned over her and promised her she would be safe, Hsu had been certain she was going to die.

She felt like she kept cheating death—something she felt she had no right to do.

"Hey." Irina stuck her head into the room. "You ready? They said we need to get going ASAP." She pronounced the acronym a bit awkwardly. "What is ASAP? I know what it means, but..."

"A-S-A-P, As Soon As Possible," Hsu explained. American idioms had made their way all over the globe, even into the labs in China and Bulgaria.

"Oh. I see." Irina wiggled her jaw and tapped at her ear. "I'm not sure how I like this implant. It's really weird not to understand the words that are coming out of my mouth. I mean, I know what I am saying, but you see the point."

Hsu nodded, "I do." She looked around the small bunk. "Okay, I'm ready."

"You're not taking any weapons?" Irina asked.

"I don't have any," Hsu pointed out. "Anyway, it's hard to hide a gun under a lab coat when you're this small. I should be able to talk my way into the facilities without needing to shoot people."

"Oh?" Irina fell into step beside her as they walked down the hallways. "What's your plan?"

Hsu grinned. "Use their biggest fear against them. They'll practically run to get into the trap—and then we can waltz in and free the shifters."

Gordes, France

Hidden on the roof underneath a heat shield, Emeric Carre watched as a black object shot into the sky.

The forest was eerily quiet, and the sound of the trucks had faded away.

Emeric considered what he had seen. The two on the roof had not been humans—a shifter and a vampire, to judge by the smell.

And they wanted to kill Gerard. More than that, they had known as soon as the helicopter started. That had been part of Emeric's plan—see what would happen if he tried to take off.

Now he knew. He would not use the helicopter. He would sneak away to join his brethren at the other facilities. And he would warn them of the people he had seen.

Who *were* they?

He had heard stories of shifters who debased themselves to become assassins for human drug lords. If they were both shifters, he would have said that these two served Hugo.

But he had never heard of a vampire doing such a thing.

A vampire involved usually meant one thing, and one thing only—that the Rules of Honor were being enforced. The vampires must have decided, in their infinite wisdom, that they would handle this. They would dispense justice, and they would take Hugo and Gerard down. When it was over, they would expect Emeric and the rest to just forgive and forget when the whole world had enabled what happened to them.

He had no intentions of letting that happen.

They *would* have their revenge.

Istaravshan, Tajikistan

"Good evening." Hsu allowed the door of the Istaravshan facility to bang open as she strode in.

Stoyan stood at one shoulder, Irina at the other. The two cousins glared at the guards as they all looked at one another.

"Who are you?" A flustered woman with ruddy cheeks and flyaway brown hair pounded down the stairs and strode up to Hsu.

"I," Hsu said, "am your salvation."

She just had to get through this without laughing.

"What the hell does that mean?" the woman demanded. "I am the administrator of this facility. Talk fast before I have you removed."

"I will leave immediately if you want." Hsu gave an artful shrug. "But you should know Gerard is on his way to this facility, and he has been instructed to have all staff executed. You have..." She checked her watch. "Seventeen minutes until the poison vents open."

A ripple of alarm spread through the group. Two of the guards dropped their weapons and turned to run—most likely to warn the rest of the facility.

"Wait!" the administrator snapped. She turned back and gave Hsu an unfriendly look. "We don't know that she's telling the truth. After all, Hugo sent word that Gerard was not to be trusted."

Shit. Hsu had forgotten that. She scrambled for a cover.

"Yes, and didn't you wonder why that was?" That should buy her a moment.

The administrator looked around at the others. No one seemed to have an answer to that.

"Why was it?" she asked finally.

"Because..." She really should think of something to say. "Gerard is now employed by one of Hugo's rivals." That worked. "And his rival wants this operation shut down *permanently*."

The woman paled. "We will lock him out of the facility."

"It is far, far too late for that," Hsu told her. "He's bringing mercenaries, and he's already hacked the facility. *I* am here to get you all out, and—God willing—shut things down and extract the experiments before irreparable damage is done to this program. So." She drew herself up. "Are you going to let me do my job, or should I leave you to your deaths? I'm happy to do either but believe me when I say that I do not intend to be here when Gerard arrives."

The administrator had been caught the moment Hsu mentioned Gerard. There had never really been a chance that she would throw Hsu out.

The woman was visibly panicked now. "How do I get everyone out in time? The experiments—"

"Focus on your staff," Hsu said simply. She forced herself to smile as she added, "It's more important that we be able to reproduce the experiments than that this set gets out."

The woman nodded in relief. She clearly considered the lives of the experiments an acceptable loss.

Hsu had to force herself not to reach out and throttle her.

"Tell your personnel to evacuate immediately. Arisha will direct them to a safe point in the forest." Hsu gestured to Arisha, who was hovering by the door. "My associates

NATALIE GREY & MICHAEL ANDERLE

and I will attempt to disable the poison vents and evacuate the experiments."

"Right away. Of course." The administrator practically ran for the elevator.

Hsu allowed herself a small smile.

Within two minutes, the stairs were full of escaping scientists and security personnel.

Irina pushed her way between them. She was trying not to lash out at them—at their monstrous selfishness, leaving the Wechselbalg to die in their cages.

She opened the first laboratory door, however, to find a scientist pinned against the back wall while wolves advanced on him.

The Wechselbalg swung their heads to look at Irina and took a sniff. They hesitated, uncertain.

Irina was also uncertain. She had seen this before.

"How did they get out of their cages?" she asked the scientists in Tajik.

"I-I let them out," he stammered.

Irina looked at the wolves. One nodded its head.

"Why?" Irina asked him sharply.

"They were going to be left to die! There's no time to evacuate them, and it wasn't right!" The man held his hands up, babbling now. "I never—never wanted to…" His voice trailed away.

"Suppose for a moment that I am not part of this corporation," she suggested. "Suppose that we're here to trick the scientists into leaving—whereupon they will be tried and possibly executed—and to free the shifters."

The man's jaw hung open. "I... What?"

"I was once one of them." Irina pointed. "At a facility in Bulgaria. I am here to get them out, and I will be one of the judges who decides if we spare *any* of the scientists. So why don't you explain to me why I shouldn't kill you, and *I* will decide if your explanation is good enough."

"I, I..." The man looked like he wanted to throw up. He took a deep breath. "I took a job here three months ago. I didn't realize what I was going to be doing until I arrived. I requested a transfer, and Administrator Nabiyev warned me that he would pretend he hadn't heard the question, but if I asked again, he would have to turn me in. He told me that no one left."

Irina frowned, "I thought the administrator was a woman."

"It is now," the scientist explained. "They thought Nabiyev was too soft, and they had him executed in front of all of us." He gulped. "But not before he told me that the local police were all in on this, and some of the international inspectors. Hugo...he bribed a lot of people."

"So you stayed," Irina said flatly.

"Yes, but not like you think! I fabricated my results, I never ran a single experiment!" He looked at her wildly. "I mapped out the facility to see how I could get out, and I was collecting documents so I could expose this place. They're over there, in that filing cabinet—I swear, go look!"

Irina walked between the press of wolf bodies and pulled open the drawer.

The papers were there, as he had said, though she

couldn't make head or tail of the technical readouts. She saw letters and emails, however, some implicating officials.

"Is what he says true?" she asked the wolves.

One of the wolves transformed into a woman. She stood up awkwardly, arms shielding her chest.

"It's true," she said. "He would talk to us. He told us that he would give a signal when we were to transform, a hand signal, like this." Her fingers fluttered. "And he would pretend to press the button, but he wouldn't really. He said if we just pretended, we would buy him time to get us out of here. We thought..." She swallowed. "We thought he might be lying, but he wasn't torturing us. So we went along with it."

Irina considered this. "All right. You all, stay here and guard him. I'm going to release the others. I'll send someone along to check his story a bit more thoroughly in a moment." She looked at the scientist. "Did anyone help you?"

"One of the guards." He jerked his head. "I think. I'm not sure. Her name's Richa. I swear she caught me talking to them one night, but she never said anything. If she had, I'd be dead."

Irina nodded. "I'll tell the others to look out for her."

Istaravshan, Tajikistan

Hsu looked around at the assembled staff. They huddled in the forest, looking for helicopters in the pale dawn sky.

"They're all in the containment area," ADAM told her. "The additional scientist and guard are still at the facility, being questioned by Stephen. I can put up the barrier here on your mark."

"Thank you, ADAM. Do it now." Hsu laced her hands behind her back and watched as energy fields sprang up to pen in the staff and guards.

Screams of panic sounded from inside the cage.

"I see you do not like being caged," Hsu said conversationally.

"What are you doing?" the administrator demanded. "Are you one of Gerard's people?"

"I am not," Hsu said evenly. Anger was beginning to beat in her blood. "I am definitely not. But you are."

The administrator sputtered, "We are not!"

"You are," Hsu accused her. "I hear from my colleagues that you were brought in after the last administrator was deemed to be 'too soft.' You questioned the staff to see if anyone had sympathies for the Wechselbalg. You had others executed."

"I had to! It was my life on the line!"

"I see. And what actions did you take to subvert the research program?" Hsu tilted her head to the side.

There was a deafening silence.

"When we gave the order to evacuate," Hsu said flatly, "*two* of you stayed behind to try to see if they could get the shifters out. Two. There are forty-one of you in front of me now. Out of forty-three...two. All of you here decided to save your own skins and leave the shifters with the chance of dying."

The people looked at one another.

"You have been judged for your actions," Hsu told them.

"Can any of you tell me truly that you had no choice, and no opportunity to disobey?"

Again, there was silence.

"ADAM. Do it."

She watched as the bodies slumped to the ground. A quick, painless death. It was better than they deserved after what they had done.

But at least it was over now.

5

QBS *ArchAngel*

Richa huddled in her bed at the end of the medical bay.

She didn't understand what was happening. First, there had been the strange announcement from Administrator Vasilieva that the facility must be evacuated due to grave danger—and to leave the experiments.

Richa wasn't about to do that.

She had arrived a month ago, in high spirits. The facility at Istaravshan was remote, of course, but the pay was excellent, and she had stopped enjoying the cities. The drinking, the late nights, never getting anywhere in her career... Remote places were nice, in any case. Richa had brought a whole suitcase full of books, some of them in English. She was excited to learn new languages.

It went to hell quickly. The first time she saw the humans in their cages, she screamed. A scientist yanked her out of the room and into a tiny broom closet.

"You can't ever let them see you like that. They kill the people

who feel sorry for the experiments."

She'd made a plan to run away, as soon as he said those words—until he reminded her that they knew where her family lived, too. *You think Administrator Nabiyev's family was spared? They weren't.*

She didn't know what to do.

She volunteered for all the late shifts, and she snuck as much food as she could into her pockets and brought it to them. She didn't know what else to do. The ones in wolf form growled at her, and once or twice she almost lost a finger, but she didn't stop.

Then one night, one of them talked to her.

He was a man with rich brown hair and eyes like midnight, and he changed back from his wolf form in front of her. She looked away from his nakedness—as much from politeness as anything, but he whispered three words to her—*Look at me.*

She looked. She saw the bruises on his skin.

Thus began the strangest friendship she had ever had. They never once spoke of what happened in the facility. They might have been two friends talking in a coffee shop, except they were whispering, in the dark, and she hid every time she saw the sweep of another guard's flashlight.

His name was Firuz, and he had a little daughter, a girl he hoped had been taken far away by her mother—he had heard that the people who ran this facility looked for whole families.

He hadn't seen her show up, but he was terrified they might be doing experiments on her at another facility.

He asked about Richa's family. She told him how her little brother had started listening to American rock music and calling everyone "dude." She told him how her little sister was convinced that, at sixteen, she was grown up enough to get married and have her own house and wanted to buy a wedding dress for when she met her perfect man. Firuz laughed when Richa told him these things, and she liked making him laugh.

None of the others ever spoke to her, but she noticed that none of them tried to hurt her or growl at her, either, after she befriended Firuz.

And when she was told to leave them behind...well, she knew she couldn't.

She was opening cages frantically when a man and a woman burst into the lab, guns drawn. Richa thought she screamed, and she knew she threw herself in front of Firuz. She didn't have a plan. She only had the certainty that somehow, against all the odds, she was going to stop them from hurting the shifters.

The woman cocked her head to the side, eyes narrowed in speculation. "Are you Richa?"

"How do you know my name?" They were going to kill her. They were going to kill her family. "Don't hurt my family! I'll—"

"We're not going to hurt you or your family," the man said gravely. He didn't look Tajik, but he spoke the language perfectly. "We are here to save these Wechselbalg, and we heard that you were doing the same."

"Oh." Richa stared at him. "I...yes. I am. You're really here to help them?"

It might be a trap, after all.

Firuz leaned and whispered, "She is like me, a shifter."

What happened next still didn't make much sense.

Richa had come out of the facility to see black egg-like vehicles hovering above the ground. Firuz pulled her into one of them and, though the egg never seemed to move, soon they were in another facility with gleaming metal corridors and a lot of people speaking English. There was an impossibly detailed mural of the earth from space that even seemed to be moving.

Footsteps approached, and a bright-eyed young tech smiled at Richa.

"You're all cleared, Ms. Boqiev."

"How does everyone here speak Tajik?" Richa demanded.

"Oh." The tech laughed. "It's the implants. They translate in real time. Now, if you don't have any other questions or concerns, you'll be brought back to Earth shortly with the rest of those recovered from the facility. We ask that you stay in this section of the ship, and that—"

"Back to Earth?"

"Of course." The tech looked confused. "Ms. Boqiev, you're on the *QBS ArchAngel*. In orbit."

Stephen and Jennifer made their way through the now-packed corridors, trying to find the easiest path to their conference room.

The sudden stench of vomit made them both wrinkle their noses. A tech hurrying by with cleanup rags gave them a guilty look. "One of the people hadn't realized they were in space. They didn't take the news all that well."

Jennifer snickered.

Hsu, Irina, Stoyan, and Arisha were waiting for them in the conference room.

"Good news," Hsu told them. "ADAM has confirmed that the bones from the facility in France were not Wechselbalg. Also, the helicopter hasn't moved—so wherever they're going, they're still in trucks."

"Good to know." Stephen nodded at her as he took a seat. "Any idea where they *are* going, ADAM?"

"My best guess is that they are going to the facility in Postojna, Slovenia. Their direction fits, and it is the closest facility by far."

Stephen frowned, tapping his fingers on the arm of the chair. "And have there been any further transmissions from Gerard? Can we confirm that he's with them?"

"No transmissions, although he appears to have tried accessing his email recently."

"I don't like that we don't know his status," Jennifer said quietly. "He could slip away from that convoy at any time and disappear."

"He wants power too much to do that," Hsu explained. "I think he really did leave Hugo to die. The two of them had been fighting, and I think Gerard realized he was helping Hugo accumulate power when he could just take it for himself. So if he got the shifters from that facility to follow him, he's not going to give them up."

Stephen sighed. "So we need to expose his lies."

Arisha shook her head. "I thought everyone knew who he was. And if they know who he is and they're still following him, then you have a major problem to sort out. Because he's got some kind of crazy hold on them—whatever he said to make them trust him, it's *good*."

Irina agreed, "She has a point."

Stephen looked out the window into the glittering black of space. "Is it possible that he's a captive? That they are using him to get into the other facilities?"

There was a stunned silence behind them.

"I think that's very possible," Jennifer said. "In which case, they would be open to knowing that we're involved."

"But if he is not their captive, they would try to kill you," Hsu reminded them. "ADAM says he is checking his email. He has not sent any sort of distress signal. And he is dangerous and charismatic. What if one of them takes pity on him and helps him escape?"

Jennifer rubbed her temples, "I just wish we knew which it was."

"I wonder if there's any of the pack left," Stephen said suddenly. "Near Gordes. If we find the pack, they might be able to tell us something about the members—or something to call them back."

"Be careful with that," Irina advised. "And don't take too long. Maybe he's just conning them into thinking he'll help them get revenge…until he can get them in range of command waves."

The table went silent.

"I'll go immediately," Stephen told them. "Hsu, Jennifer, Stoyan, Arisha—you did well at the last facility. Would you want to go to one of the others and begin evacuating it?"

He knew that things might go south, but he also knew that the staff at the facilities were cowards, only too eager to save their own skins at the expense of others. And the idea of leaving the Wechselbalg any longer than he had to was agony.

He looked at Jennifer. *Are you okay with this?*

Of course. Jennifer nodded her head at him with a small smile.

"Irina, come with me now. Your experience may convince the pack to be more open, then we can see about intercepting the caravan. We don't have much time before they reach Postojna."

Outskirts of Gordes, France

Two hours later, Emeric Carre approached the small airstrip just as a tired man hauled the gates open. The man muttered a *bonjour* without even looking up. He wanted to get this over with and go back to his breakfast, Emeric knew.

Humans were so weak.

He tried not to sneer as he made his way through the tiny building. He still needed these humans, after all, as much as it pained him.

Not forever, he assured himself. Just for now.

He thought about his escape from Gordes. How he'd held the heat shielding over himself, as he'd crept carefully through the facility and out into the forest. The people who had come to the facility, the vampire and its pet Wechselbalg (Emeric's lip curled in disgust at this) clearly had impressive technology at their beck and call. Even if that technology did not include infrared, and they were not still scanning the facility, it was better to overestimate them.

After all, why would Hugo stock such shields in his facilities unless he knew they might be useful? After the staff had been disposed of, Emeric and the others had done a thorough inventory, finding guns and other technology.

It was only in the bustle of the town that he dropped the heat shielding and reluctantly left it in an alleyway. It was too heavy to keep carrying. Then he headed for the airport—a structure on the outskirts of town, barely deserving the name.

The building seemed to have only three employees—the man at the gate, and two more at the desk, where a receptionist chatted with a man in rougher clothes. The pilot, Emeric guessed.

Good.

Both of them looked over, half-interested. Emeric had their full attention when he slid a stack of dirty bills onto the desk. Their eyes widened when the bills were joined by another stack the same size.

"*Oui, monsieur?*" The receptionist eyed Emeric with a new appreciation.

"I need a flight to Khachmaz," Emeric requested pleasantly. "I have money for fuel, and bribes if ordered to stop." He pushed one stack of bills forward. "This is for you, to make sure you don't have any troubles explaining why the plane couldn't be here today…and if you happen to provide official verification of our flight plan, so much the better."

The receptionist took the stack of bills so quickly that it seemed to disappear into thin air. She smiled, cloyingly sweet. "Of course, sir."

Emeric slid the other stack of bills to the pilot. "And this is for you. Compensation for this flight, for any other days of work missed getting back, and maybe a few tune-ups on the plane."

"*Merci, monsieur,*" the man murmured, evidently pleased. He tucked the bills into his coat. "Khachmaz...."

"Azerbaijan."

"It will be a long trip, no?" The pilot tapped his mouth speculatively. "Perhaps we will stop and get another plane. Warmer. Faster."

"Do whatever you wish." Emeric nodded to the pilot's pocket. "I leave it in your capable hands."

The pilot smiled.

Neither of them asked why he was going to Khachmaz. The money said clearly that he wanted no such questions, and their sleek smiles told him that they had made deals like this often—if, perhaps, never for so far a destination.

As Emeric ate a small breakfast, provided with another cloying smile by the receptionist, he allowed himself to be pleased.

The team would go to Postojna, and melt into the woods and wait for him. He, meanwhile, would recruit the captives at Khachmaz, Naftalan, and Naryn. The plane would be useful—as long as the pilot was as discreet as he seemed. If not, Emeric could find someone else willing to bring him across borders with no questions asked.

When he had his army assembled—the executions would begin. First, the officials who had turned a blind eye. Then, the vampire who wanted Emeric to accept some higher law of justice than simple revenge.

And last, the humans who thought they were better than Wechselbalg.

The world would kneel at Emeric's feet, or it would feel his wrath.

6

Gordes, France

It was mid-morning as Stephen and Irina made their way through Gordes.

Stephen walked confidently. In some ways, he felt most at home in these smaller towns, with the older buildings and the narrow streets. These smaller towns resembled the world he remembered...right down to the way the Wechselbalg hid in plain sight.

If he was lucky, anyway.

Stephen looked for the telltale signs—a less fashionable part of town, the buildings a bit more run-down, the streets a bit dirtier and narrower. For humans, to whom acceptance was a vital part of survival, it was considered dangerous to live in the bad part of town. People would tell their children not to play with yours. Everyone would know your name and might not give you work.

But that sort of thing was better for the Wechselbalg. Close friendships led to secrets being exposed, and those secrets could result in a witch hunt. As a Wechselbalg, it was better to rely only on the pack.

It was not long before they heard the faint sound of footsteps and turned to see a young man shadowing them.

The man was tall and broad-shouldered, very muscular, and seemed instinctively disposed to glower.

Stephen smiled. He adjusted his cuffs as he strolled over to the man and was pleased to see the man's face flicker uncertainly. He was clearly used to people running.

"Good morning," Stephen said pleasantly.

The man stared at him silently. His nostrils flared.

"Ah, yes." Stephen smiled more broadly. "You know what I am, I think, and you know what to do."

Still, the man said nothing, but an involuntary flicker of his eyes betrayed him.

Stephen followed the flicker and saw a house with a blue door. He looked back. "Is that where your Alpha lives?"

"No," the man replied instantly, then, a second too late, "I don't know what you mean."

"You need to get better at lying," Stephen advised him. He turned toward the door and paused. "But, lest you be worried, I mean you no harm. I am bringing word of members of your pack who were taken from their homes."

The man gulped. "You found them? At the facility?"

All of his recalcitrance was gone. The promise of information clearly thrilled him. Thick fingers clenched around Stephen's arm—not out of malice, but out of desperation.

"Yes." Stephen waited for the man to remove his hand, focusing on his patience. This man's agony was more important than a wrinkled suit.

"Why don't you take me to your Alpha?" Stephen suggested.

"Yes, of course. At once. Sir."

"How do you know how to do all of this?" Irina asked Stephen curiously.

"Centuries of practice," Stephen told her. He paused. "Although I like it better now, I think."

"How do you mean?" she asked him as they followed their guide a bit more slowly.

"What he just did—touching me like that—is something that would once have been forbidden. I like that the rules are more relaxed about some things now." Stephen smiled. "Though no one gets a free pass."

Irina smiled. She had once been over-awed by this man and did not understand how Jennifer could be so comfortable in his presence. Her whole life, she had been taught to respect vampires—and, if possible, not be noticed by them. Mothers taught their children that it was better to keep one's head down and follow the rules than risk coming to the attention of the Patriarch.

And no matter how much those same children argued that the Patriarch didn't care about a Wechselbalg that stayed up past their bedtime or refused to eat their vegetables, there was still a superstitious thrill of fear every time someone mentioned him.

But now that Irina had met Stephen and Bethany Anne, she was rethinking her worries.

It turned out vampires just really, *really* didn't like people absolving themselves of responsibility, or messing with innocents.

And Irina couldn't find any problem with that.

Postojna, Slovenia

"All right." Hsu smiled at the others in the Pod. "Does anyone else want to be the self-important bitch this time?"

Jennifer laughed. "I do like the sound of that, but I don't think anyone is going to believe you're a bodyguard. You're barely five feet tall."

"I will have you know," Hsu said with great dignity, "that I am very dangerous when I need to be."

"Uh-huh. And I'm guessing you have a good element of surprise." Jennifer was still laughing. "Plus, I like seeing your self-important bitch act."

Hsu grinned. She had seen so many self-important party officials come to visit her facility back in China that she had plenty of inspiration to draw on for her act.

She had learned that it was essential to act as though it was completely unbelievable that anyone would question you. It was also important to believe that everyone in the system was dishonest—that the administrators, therefore, were very susceptible to blackmail. She had seen how to hint at illicit dealings without any details, causing her targets to believe that she knew a lot more about them than she really did.

As much as she hated to admit it, she enjoyed play-acting as all those people she despised.

The Pod let them out in a stand of trees where they waited for ADAM's confirmation that there were no signs of alarm from the facility.

They approached from the road. Hsu's badge had the

gates sliding open before anyone even appeared at the doors of the facility itself.

Unfortunately, when they did, they were armed and clearly not willing to accept unexpected visitors.

Crap.

"Who are you?" one of the guards yelled.

Hsu drew herself up to her full height, "Your readiness is commendable," she called across the yard. "Hugo will be pleased."

The men wavered, the barrels of their guns swinging slightly as they looked at one another.

Hsu announced. "I am Chief Administrator Zhang. I have been sent by Hugo to oversee the facilities as they dismantle operations."

There was a small flurry of activity, and the door opened to let a swarthy man through. He wore a suit beneath his lab coat and looked displeased to see Hsu.

"*Chief* Administrator?" he asked. He switched to Catalan the next minute: "Why would Hugo appoint a foreigner to be his chief administrator? You are lying."

Hsu rolled her eyes before she could stop herself, then decided that this was exactly what an official would do, as well.

"Your prejudice against foreigners is noted," she informed him. She decided not to point out that, as a Spanish man assigned to a Slovenian facility, he was also a foreigner. "Hugo, however, is not as foolish as you. Should you wish to rise in this organization, I suggest you spend less time worrying about heritage, and more time worrying about your job performance."

The administrator flushed angrily, and Hsu held up a hand to forestall any angry outbursts.

"I do not have any information on Hugo's opinion of your work. If you feel you should have my job, you are of course welcome to discuss this with him when you return to Spain. *However*, we will first need to shutter this facility."

The man looked at her hatefully but shut his mouth.

"Please accompany me to my office," he suggested. It was clear that every pleasant word pained him to speak. "Your guards may remain *outside*."

"My chief of security will accompany me," Hsu replied, trying to act as carelessly arrogant as the party officials she remembered. "There are important matters she will need to be present for." She gave a tiny nod to Jennifer.

The administrator seemed very much like he wanted to object, but he knew it was a reasonable request.

Hsu swept into the facility behind him—Jennifer at one shoulder, and they walked through the hallways in stony silence.

It was only once they were in the administrator's office with the door closed securely behind them that the man turned to her with a nasty smile.

"So, *Chief Administrator Zhang*, let us be honest with one another."

Hsu forced herself to keep a bored expression on her face, although she felt a sudden chill. At her shoulder, Jennifer stood lazily, arms crossed, but Hsu knew from experience that the woman was ready to leap into action at any moment.

"I fear something has happened to Hugo," the administrator admitted quietly. "Perhaps he is being coerced in some way."

"He is not in any way being coerced," Hsu told him confidently. "I can assure you of that. And I can also assure you that he is in no danger."

After all, it was hard to be in danger when one was already dead.

The administrator sat back in his chair.

"Your caution is, again, commendable," Hsu assured him. "I understand that Hugo's transmission about Gerard must have caused some distress."

The administrator watched her carefully.

"However, other than that unfortunate falling out, there is little reason for concern."

"So you wouldn't mind..." The administrator said, reaching out for a button, "if we made a quick video call to Hugo to confirm that?"

Gordes, France

Stephen was led into the sitting room of a house that was, indeed, quite nice. Though it was clear that the owners were not affluent, it was far from the wreck that the outside would suggest.

It was not long before a man with hair so white it appeared silver ducked into the room. Though he was getting older, he still walked strongly, and his grip was firm when he shook Stephen's hand.

"I am Jean-Marc Carre," he announced.

Stephen introduced himself and Irina, and the three of

them sat as the surly-looking young man came to hover at the back of the room.

"I will guess that you are aware of the laboratories on the outskirts of town," Stephen offered.

Jean-Marc looked, abruptly, far older. His shoulders slumped. "Yes," he answered quietly. "And you say you have news?"

Stephen could see that the Alpha did not believe that it would be good news. He had long since given up thinking that things might change for the better. The younger man, however, still had hope.

"Last night we learned—my team and I—that the human staff and scientists had been killed, and that the Wechselbalg were gone."

A new thought occurred to him now. What if the bodies they found were only a portion of guard staff? What if Gerard had called in more mercenaries, and the trucks held cages to transport the Wechselbalg to a new facility? ADAM had had a short gap in satellite coverage, even after rerouting a few satellites, and it was possible that cages had been carried out during that time.

Not knowing was maddening.

The Alpha stared at him. It was clear that his thoughts were moving along the same lines at Stephen's.

Irina cleared her throat, trying to find words. "I was in one of the facilities like this one, sir."

"What—" The Alpha's voice broke. "What happened to you there?"

"I'm not going to say." Irina went to sit beside him on the couch. "It won't help anyone to dwell on the past. All I can say is that after everything, when I escaped, I didn't want to go back to my pack. I knew that, like you, they would feel guilty and they would want to know what happened. I devoted myself to bringing justice to the people who did this. I think perhaps that's what happened here. It's one explanation, anyway."

Jean-Marc pushed himself up, away from the dark-haired girl with the strange accent, away from the vampire.

The people who ran this facility, whoever they were, had snatched away members of his pack so quickly that there was no chance to protect them: a young man helping a farmer, a little girl playing in the street, a young mother who had gone to the market for oranges.

Twice, whole families had been taken, and the other packs nearby sent emissaries to say that their people were missing as well.

There had been a media circus, one that Jean-Marc tried to hide from as much as possible.

None of the humans had the good sense to suspect the facility that had just been set up nearby...but, then again, none of the rest of them could smell blood on the evening breeze. So they gave interviews pleading for the return of their family members.

Jean-Marc had given no interviews to the press because he knew he would speak the truth—the humans were dead. Someone wanted to experiment on Wechselbalg, and humans were useless. Especially humans who had seen things they shouldn't see.

Now this woman was telling him that he should not even ask what had happened to his family—but that it had been so bad that she, having been subjected to the same, feared to see her own kin ever again.

NATALIE GREY & MICHAEL ANDERLE

And then the truth came to him.

"You said you devoted yourself to bringing justice to these people." He did not turn around.

"Yes." The girl sounded uncertain.

"That is where they have gone."

He heard the silence and knew that they were trying to figure out how to tell him not to get his hopes up.

"You don't understand." He turned back to them. "My son, Emeric. He was taken." He saw the pain in their eyes, and he struggled for the words to explain this. "He was always resentful of the life we lived. He did not like that we were forced to keep to the shadows for our own protection. He said many distressing things over the years—that we were better than they were, that we should take our rightful place at the head of society. I never agreed with him, and eventually, he stopped saying those things.

"But I know he never stopped believing them. If he suffered terrible things at their hands and he still lives, he is going to take vengeance. And it..." His voice cracked. "You cannot allow it. I cannot. I must go to him."

"It's too dangerous," the man replied at once. "We think he may have been lied to by a man named Gerard Cordova, a human who worked in this program. He betrayed the man who started it and may be trying to collect the army for himself. I fear he is telling them lies to trick them into doing his dirty work for him."

Jean-Marc's hands clenched. "I cannot think Emeric would trust such a man. I cannot even think he would give this Gerard the time to speak. If you want my thoughts—truly want them—then I must tell you I think Gerard is dead if he ever met my son." He paused, shuddering. "And I think my son is going to do something terrible. He must be stopped."

Irina and Stephen looked sharply at one another, but before they could respond, a voice spoke in Stephen's ear:

"There's a problem in Postojna," ADAM told him. "The director wanted to confirm face to face with Hugo that the facility should be shut down. I cut the call off, of course, but it looks like it will be a fight. If you want to be there for that, you should leave now."

7

Gordes, France

A Pod was waiting for Stephen and Irina on the edge of town as they hurried away from Jean-Marc Carre's house.

"ADAM, can you mimic Hugo's voice?" Stephen stepped back to allow Irina to get into the Pod first.

"Yes, I can do that. I assume that you have a plan to explain why it will be only a voice call and not a video call, as the administrator intends?"

"I do. In fact..." Stephen considered. "Could you make my voice sound like Hugo's while transmitting it?"

"Yes."

"Put a call through, then."

"One moment." There was a pause.

Irina settled back in her seat. She was endlessly interested by the ability of Bethany Anne's team to problem solve. Instead of just going in, guns blazing, Stephen planned to talk his way out of this. It was not a simple solution, but it would keep the captive Wechselbalg from being caught in the crossfire.

But Stephen was still ready for a fight if there was no other option.

She checked her own weapons carefully, being sure to point them away from Stephen at a specific point on the wall. ADAM had explained to her that some Pods now came with a square of material, designed by Jean Dukes—a woman Irina had never met, though everyone seemed to speak of her with reverence—that would absorb gunfire. That way, the inhabitants of the Pod could do last-minute weapons check without worrying that gunfire would reverberate around the Pod if there were a malfunction.

"Patching you into the call," ADAM informed Stephen.

"Thank you." Stephen waited until a voice answered.

"*Si?*"

"Good morning, Gomez." Stephen was amused to hear his voice coming out sounding exactly like Hugo's.

Amused, but unnerved. The man really did sound not only relentlessly self-absorbed but also a bit on the whiny side.

"Good morning, Mr. Marcari." The administrator's voice was unctuous.

"What is the meaning of this, Gomez?" Stephen demanded.

"I beg your pardon, Mr. Marcari?" The administrator sounded flustered now. "I have an unknown woman in my facility—"

"Did I not make myself clear?" Stephen unconsciously folded his arms, the way he would if he were staring someone down. He saw Irina's grin and had to stifle a laugh. "I informed you, did I not, that the research was to be discontinued and that I would send personnel to extract the experiments?"

"Yes, sir, absolutely, you did, sir, but—"

Stephen seized on the fatal 'but,' "But when I sent personnel, as I told you I would, you decided to question me?"

"No, sir, I absolutely do not mean to question you!" The voice was full of panic now.

"Am I also going to find out that you have been dealing with Gerard Cordova?" Stephen demanded. "Have you disobeyed those instructions, as well?"

"No!"

"So what is the meaning of this?" Stephen returned to the original point. What would Hugo complain about now? "Gerard's betrayal has put me in mortal danger, and you have compromised my security by forcing me to call you."

"Sir, I cannot apologize enough. I meant only to verify that—"

"That *what*?" Stephen snapped, cutting the man off on purpose. He had learned that when people were guilty and cut off mid-sentence, they seemed to believe somehow that they could have talked their way out of things if given half a chance. Not being given a chance to speak drove them into a frenzy. "I will be sending more personnel to aid in the extraction. They will be there in a few minutes."

"In..." Stephen could see the man in his mind's eye. The administrator, ensconced in a remote facility, was no doubt standing up to check the windows right now. "So soon?"

"Gomez, I have technology at my disposal that you

could not begin to understand. I expect you to cooperate with these officials, do you understand me? I will have them report to me on your behavior—and if I am not satisfied, I am afraid I will be unable to recommend you for any new positions. In fact, I am sure I will need to see you in person to discuss your failure in judgment."

"Sir, I will, of course, assist the personnel in any way—"

Stephen cut the call off with a grimace and a chuckle. "That should do it," he said to Irina.

Postojna, Slovenia

The door of the Pod slid open.

"I took the liberty of leaving you at the same place as the last Pod," ADAM announced.

"Thank you, ADAM." Stephen stepped down and offered Irina a hand. "We'll take it from here. What is Hsu calling herself?"

"Chief Administrator Zhang. No one else has provided names."

"Hmm. I think I will be Associate Administrator Cormanescu." Stephen shot a grin at Irina.

"Pleased to meet you, Associate Administrator." Irina fluttered her lashes. "I'm just the hired muscle, don't mind me, I don't need a name."

Stephen laughed as they made their way around the fence to the outside of the facility. "Now the fun begins."

Hsu sat, a cup of truly terrible tea cradled in her hands as Administrator Gomez fluttered around her.

Her link with ADAM had provided her a front row seat to the man's conversation with Stephen. He had insisted that she take his seat behind the desk, had brought her the tea and some refreshments, and was now telling her just how much he admired her work.

She appreciated that Stephen had made the man significantly more pliant, but he was also annoying her enough that she wanted to backhand him. She amused herself by picturing that, in detail, until there was a flurry of activity in the hallway and Stephen appeared, Irina at one shoulder.

"Associate Administrator Cormanescu," ADAM informed her.

"Ah." Hsu smiled. "Cormanescu. Gomez said someone would be joining us." She shot a not-altogether-impressed look at the administrator, who was now fluttering around Stephen.

"Simply let me know how I can best assist you," Gomez requested eagerly.

"Which floors are security locked with electronic doors with *round* handles?" Hsu asked him.

"I'm..." The administrator's brow furrowed. "I'm not sure I follow."

"Electronic doors will allow us to keep the doors locked even if keys are used," Hsu explained, making sure to sound annoyed. "And round door handles are impossible for a wolf paw to manipulate. Do you intend to ask questions at *every* step of this process, Administrator Gomez?"

The administrator gulped. "N-no."

"Chief Administrator Zhang is asking you to make sure that your personnel will be safe," Stephen explained, in his deathly quiet voice. "While we have confidence in our abilities to extract the experiments, the fact remains that Wechselbalg are inherently dangerous and the experiment has been shut down for a reason."

At this, the administrator puffed up his chest. "We had been making enormous strides at this facility. I believe that we would have fulfilled Mr. Marcari's mandate, if—"

"You do?" Hsu swiveled the chair to stare at him. "And would you stake your reputation on that, Mr. Gomez?" She deliberately left out his title. "Or are you simply saying it because you know the program has been shut down and you will never be asked to prove it?"

Gomez gulped again.

Hsu stood up and gestured imperiously to the phone on the administrator's desk. He hurried over and gave the order for everyone to withdraw to Floor Eight.

"Send me a confirmation as soon as you have the correct count of employees, and we will make sure the doors are sealed," Hsu announced.

"Yes, ma'am." The administrator bobbed his head nervously and hurried to the door.

There, he turned. "If I may—I know I shouldn't ask questions, ma'am—but if—well, that is to say, what will happen to the Wechselbalg?"

Hsu's eyebrows shot up in surprise. It was a moment of humanity she had not expected from the man. She decided to confirm, just to be sure.

"In your opinion, what should happen? You have worked with them for some time."

"I simply don't think it's safe for them to be released," the man replied reluctantly. "Obviously, it would be terrible to suggest execution, but..."

"But?" Stephen asked delicately. Hsu could see the rage beginning, deep below the surface.

"But I cannot think of any other option, save lifetime imprisonment. They would surely hunt down the staff of the facility—they are not, after all, without intelligence."

"Thank you for your recommendation," Hsu managed. She could feel her heart beating fast with anger. "We will take it into account. Please continue your evacuation."

This was a good test, she decided. Insinuate that the shifters would be killed and give them a chance to protest.

In the administrator's absence, they waited in silence. None of them wanted to take the chance that their words would be overheard.

Finally, the phone rang.

Hsu picked it up, "Yes?"

"We are all on Floor Eight," Administrator Gomez told her. "We will remain here until we receive further instructions."

"Good," Hsu replied simply.

On the other side of the room, Stephen subvocalized, "ADAM? Lock them in."

Sabina huddled in her cage.

There had been a sudden spate of activity a few minutes back, guards posted at the doors of the labs and the scientists looking tense and worried. But then they had all disappeared. All of them.

Her eyes went to the vents at the top of the room, and she swallowed hard.

They all knew the vents' purpose. They emitted poison, to kill them if they ever got free. Once, Sabina had taken a grim pleasure in the fact that the poison would also kill the scientists. She sometimes saw the scientists look worriedly at the vents as well. They knew they were expendable.

Except, now they were all gone. Two days ago, the experiments had stopped, and today they had all disappeared.

Sabina was terrified.

The door opened, and a woman with a bouncy brown ponytail and perfectly tailored clothing slipped into the lab. She smiled at all of them.

"I am Jennifer," she said in Slovenian. "Here, smell. I am also Wechselbalg."

She held out her hand to one of the nearest cages, and Goron, one of the oldest shifters in the facility, padded forward on wolf paws to sniff her. He transformed immediately.

"She speaks the truth," he agreed cautiously.

The woman named Jennifer pressed a button on the desk, and every cage clicked open.

"The staff of this facility have been apprehended and will be dealt with. However, first, we must get all of you to our headquarters for medical treatment. I work for an organization named TQB. We were the ones behind the message that stopped the experiments, and we will be releasing all of the facilities."

"And the staff are where?" Goron asked. He stepped out of his cage and rotated his neck, taking a deep breath as he stood upright and unshackled for the first time in months.

"They are imprisoned now," the woman replied firmly. "They will be judged—and not leniently."

The man vibrated with anger; he clearly wanted nothing more than to go up the stairs and slaughter the staff.

"Are there any," Jennifer asked softly, "who have been kind to you? Who you think have been sabotaging the experiments, or who have pretended to experiment on you but have not truly done so?"

All of them laughed, even Sabina.

"Of course not," Goron spat, answering for all of them. "Why would you ask such a thing?"

"At some other facilities, scientists and guards helped the shifters and planned escapes with them." Jennifer smiled sadly. "It sounds as if that is not the case here. Please, follow me. We will get you to our ship, the *Arch-Angel*, where you will be treated for all injuries."

Outside, Hsu watched as Wechselbalg hurried to the Pods. Like Irina, they had long since become inured to being naked, and they had no shame in it—they only shivered slightly in the wind.

Some, it seemed, had argued with the mandate that they should not harm the staff of the facilities. They wanted revenge, and the shifters in each lab had said the same thing: there was no one here who had tried to flout the rules or keep them safe. They had been treated with nothing but contempt.

Stephen spoke adamantly to those who wished to stay. The smiling, affable man had disappeared entirely. When he enforced his Queen's justice, he did not bend, and he did not compromise. He would not allow them to stay here and endanger themselves for the sake of revenge.

They were not pleased, that was clear.

Hsu was afraid that they would rebel and take matters into their own hands, but the old habits seemed to run deep. They accepted Stephen's declaration and were assured that once they were back on Earth, they would have the chance to join TQB if they wished.

When he told them about Irina's choice, however, the mood changed.

Goron actually went to kneel before Irina.

"I grieve that your own alpha was so weak," he told her. "I am here because I followed my lost pack members to try to free them. Your alpha failed to protect you, and you should not bear any guilt for leaving." He stood and looked at Stephen. "It is a different world than the one I grew up in. Perhaps I do not know how best to lead any longer— not when every human carries a recording device and those across the globe can connect to share stories of shifters they have seen. It is becoming more dangerous for our kind."

"Only you may decide what to do with that information," Stephen replied courteously, "as long as you remain alpha of your pack. However, know that all who join us will be treated with respect. We will speak again on the *ArchAngel*. When you decide what to do, let me know."

Hsu shoved her hands in her pockets and strode away.

She wasn't angry, not really. She was sad. Not since she was a child had she felt such loyalty as the Wechselbalg felt to one another. She did not wish to return to the forced loyalty of the Pack or the frightened obedience of the labs...but the truth was that she had never felt a part of TQB, either.

She was a woman without honor, and she had failed twice in her quest to reclaim it. Never had she seen any end for herself but death.

But now...now, every time she joked with Irina or Stoyan, every time she listened to one of Arisha's stories or pretended to be an administrator with Stephen, she felt the fervent wish to be part of something more.

She wanted to belong somewhere.

She just wasn't sure she had the right to.

She bent her head against the winter wind and blinked the tears out of her eyes. She was not going to break down and cry, she told herself firmly. She was going to be strong. She was going to stay with the group until they were done dismantling Hugo's organization, and then she would speak privately to Stephen.

He would dispense the Queen's justice without cruelty. It was, perhaps, more than she deserved, but she was weak. She would ask for it to be quick. She would disappear quietly, and Stephen could tell whatever story he chose.

She nodded to herself. It was a good plan.

She looked around. She'd made it halfway around the edge of the facility on her walk, and she could hear the others calling her name.

As she turned to go back, however, she heard the growl

of a wolf. The next thing she knew, she was tumbling over and over into the dirt, hot breath in her face and yellow eyes boring into hers as the wolf crouched over her.

8

Postojna, Slovenia

The Wechselbalg growled deep in her throat.

This was clearly a shifter, not an ordinary wolf. A wolf, Hsu knew, would never have attacked unless she was starving, and when she attacked, she would attack quickly. This being wanted to terrify her.

"I am with the ones who are evacuating you," she choked out.

The wolf tilted her head and growled again.

"If you come with me, you will be able to smell the other Wechselbalg to see that what I am saying is true," Hsu told her. "You will not be hurt. We will give you medical treatment, and we will make those who cid this to you pay."

The wolf snarled at that and leaped free, and her claws gouged a hole in Hsu's shoulder. She screamed at the sharp, unexpected pain and struggled to sit up pressing a

77

hand over the wound. It was the same shoulder Gerard had shot her in.

The shifter changed back. The woman was too thin, and though there were no bruises or scars on her skin, she had clearly been mistreated. There was no mistaking the haunted look in her eyes.

Hsu winced, trying to find the strength to breathe. Blood was welling up in her wound.

"I'm Hsu," she said. "What's your name?"

The woman gave a snort. "Like you care."

"I do. This is the fourth facility I've helped release," Hsu told her. "Well, the third. In the first one, I was…lucky. One of the Wechselbalg helped me escape with her."

"Then she's a fool," the woman told her dismissively. "But since you asked, I'm Sidonie. And *you* can help by leaving the rest of the facilities the hell alone. Who do you think you are to take charge of this? You're ruining everything."

Hsu frowned at her, not understanding. She stood up and unbuttoned her lab coat, passing it over.

"Do you want something to wear?"

The woman crossed her arms. She tried to look unimpressed, but finally snatched the coat. She buttoned it angrily and pursed her lips at the blood on the shoulder.

Hsu refrained from mentioning the blood was her own fault.

"Look," Hsu said finally. "I'm not in charge. Stephen is. He's—"

"The vampire?"

Hsu blinked. "What? No, Stephen's not a—vampires don't—"

Sidonie rolled her eyes. "You really don't know anything, do you? That's what he is. He's acting on behalf of the *Matriarch.*" Her voice was heavy with contempt.

"Bethany Anne?" Hsu asked.

"Whatever she calls herself. The woman who replaced Michael." Sidonie lifted one shoulder, trying to look like she didn't care, but her jaw was clenched. "And you shouldn't help them."

"Why not?" Hsu demanded. "They're the ones who are freeing the facilities. No one else had a chance against Hugo, but they took him down, and they're dismantling everything."

"And robbing us of true justice!" the woman hissed.

There was a shout, and the rest of the team came bounding around the side of the building. At the sight of blood on Hsu's shoulder, Jennifer looked sharply at the woman.

In Slovenian, she asked, "Are you from this facility?"

"I'm French," the woman snapped contemptuously. "And no. And why don't *you* all pack up and go home?"

The words were rude, and Hsu was sure that was intentional, but the woman looked almost frightened as she stared Stephen down.

"No," Stephen answered calmly. "Not until the facilities are freed."

"*We* will free them," Sidonie told him. "We don't need you for that."

"You needed us to take Hugo down," Jennifer replied tightly. "You needed us to send the fake message from him saying that the project was over. You needed someone to shut down the poison vents, didn't you? Those wouldn't have worked even if they'd tried to use them—that was us."

Sidonie looked troubled at this, but she shook her head and forged on.

"Maybe you helped. But justice isn't yours to give out, it's ours. We were the ones who were imprisoned here."

"So join us," Irina exclaimed suddenly. In a way, she understood this woman's furious resolve. She didn't want to be saved. "I was in one of the facilities too, in Bulgaria. I joined Stephen and the others because my pack would not aid me in seeking justice."

"Well, that's *your* pack." Sidonie looked unimpressed. "*My* pack *is* seeking justice."

"If your Alpha is Jean-Marc Carre, you should know that he has asked me to do what I must to bring justice." Stephen's voice was even, but it had an unmistakable air of command. "As well as keep the peace."

Sidonie flinched at the mention of Jean-Marc, but at Stephen's closing words, her face hardened.

"Keep the peace," she repeated bitterly. "Why? What did peace ever do for us? We lived in little hovels on the outskirts of town. We eked out an existence, we never had the freedom to go wherever we wanted—be what we were. We were always hiding. Peace never did anything but hurt us."

"The peace," Stephen shot back sharply, "kept you alive. If humans knew of shifters, there would be a witch hunt. Your line would have been ended five times over by now, and if you somehow managed to make it to here—you'd only wind up in a government lab. You're lucky that everyone in the world thinks shifters are nothing more than fairy-tale stories."

"All my life, I've heard that story," Sidonie's fists clenched. "And you know what it is? A lie. A lie meant to make the Wechselbalg accept someone else's rule, make them slink around, and spend their time hiding—so they didn't realize they were actually more powerful than the fucking *Patriarch*."

Stephen's jaw clenched.

Jennifer's hand was on his chest, pressing him back before he realized he'd even taken a step forward.

"Listen," Jennifer said tightly, "that isn't how it works anymore. And it wasn't why Michael did what he did, either. We lived outside the normal world, we couldn't depend on them to protect us or dispense justice. We *needed* someone to do that. Every society needs that."

"And why him, huh?" Sidonie threw a glance at Stephen, raking over him with her eyes. "Why did he get to make his little pets like *this* one and send them around to do his bidding? Why did we have to obey them? We didn't choose that."

"Stephen is Michael's brother," Jennifer argued heatedly. "And Michael was the first—of *all* of us. Do you know what we really are?"

"Jennifer." Stephen managed the one word. He shook his head. No matter how angry he was, no matter how he wanted to see this woman hear the truth from Jennifer's lips, now was not the time for this particular revelation.

It was Irina, surprisingly, who broke the silence.

"People were dying," she explained quietly. "If Stephen and Bethany Anne had decided that you were right, that they should just step back and let people in the Unknown World choose their leaders, what would have happened? No one would have been strong enough to take Hugo down. TQB had resources no one else had. You can't believe that they should have looked the other way and waited for you all to break out. I *know* what happens when you wait like that. People die. I'm the only one from my facility who survived."

Sidonie shuddered. She looked away, hands clenched.

Finally, her voice low, she muttered, "I don't care. You're right. But it doesn't change *now*. You've done what you needed to do. The facilities are waiting to be dismantled. We can handle this from here."

"And then?" Stephen asked. His calm demeanor was back. He shook his head. "I am sure that Emeric will lead you and your new pack in battle just as capably as any of my fighters." He shot Jennifer a warning look not to snort derisively. "But what will come after? Jean-Marc spoke to me of Emeric's beliefs."

"Emeric sees the truth!" Sidonie spat.

"Ah." Stephen nodded. He hadn't been sure that Emeric was in charge and had hoped to lure Sidonie into confirming that piece of information. "And no doubt he believes he is smarter than Gerard."

Sidonie, however, only frowned at that. "Who?" She shook her head impatiently. "Look. You need to accept that you are not the ones who have been wronged by this. You need to leave this to us."

"No," Stephen answered simply. "I would be happy to have Emeric's support, but the Queen I serve is the only one who has the resources to see this through. She will not abdicate responsibility, knowing that it would lead to deaths."

"Her actions now have led to enemies," Sidonie threatened.

"My Queen has many enemies, but those enemies do not wish for peace."

Sidonie stared him down with pure hatred.

"Go to Emeric," Stephen advised. "Tell him what I have said. Tell him to contact his father. If it is justice that he wants, then he shall have it if he works with us."

"You would deny him his own justice," Sidonie muttered, ill-tempered.

"I would *deny* him the chance to wreak destruction on the human world," Stephen snapped. His temper was reaching a breaking point. "I do not long for a world without humans, and neither does my Queen." He took a deep breath. "Go to Emeric. See what he says. Tell him I will await his response."

QBS *ArchAngel*

"I don't get it," Arisha mused later. She was slumped in a chair, legs kicking over one arm of it. "Why won't they join up with us?"

"Because they think we have no right." Hsu looked at her calmly. "They think that the ones who were wronged should be the ones to choose how justice is dispensed—and mete it out."

"That's not how *any* society works." Stoyan voiced, coming to stand behind Arisha's chair. He smiled down at her and took her hand before he looked at Hsu. "Vigilante justice leads to chaos."

"The people we killed at Velingrad, and in Spain, and here—" Hsu paused. *"Did* we kill the ones here? Did anyone remember to do that?"

"It was done." Stephen came into the room and nodded gravely to her. "They were judged. They pleaded for their lives but offered only that they wanted to live—no reason for what they did, and no apology. They understood that they should die, and they did: by the poison they had set aside for the Wechselbalg." He looked grimly satisfied as he took a seat with the group.

Hsu nodded. Her own sense of guilt coiled within her, and she looked around the room at all of them.

"Do you understand, though? Think about me, especially." She forced herself to meet Irina's eyes. "Why should I be allowed to dispense justice? I didn't suffer from the torture, I was the torturer. And yet I am the one there, destroying the facilities. Doesn't that seem wrong?"

"Hsu." Stephen's voice brooked no argument. "We have all failed in our lives. You may have failed at Sofia. Yet, if you say those wronged should choose, why do you not accept Irina's choice to save you? We are judged by what we do. You failed, and that failure inspired you to become an instrument of justice. I once failed both my brother and my Queen, and I was given a second chance. You must accept yours. No more of this." He looked her in the eyes. "Please."

Hsu looked away, and a few seconds later, a hand slipped around her fingers and squeezed gently. She looked up to see Arisha.

"Besides," Arisha joked, "you wouldn't want to leave us without Chief Administrator Zhang, would you? The woman's a Grade A, ice cold *bitch* and I just love watching her make the administrators squirm."

Despite herself, Hsu laughed, as did the others.

"You should have seen her in that dude's office." Jennifer was laughing. "I'll see if I can get ADAM to pull the tapes. 'Are you going to ask questions *every* step of the way, Gomez?'" She tried to mimic Hsu's icy demeanor and failed as she was still giggling.

"Oh, stop it," Hsu muttered. She could feel her cheeks flushing, and she pressed her hands over them to hide her face.

"No, seriously, how do you do it?" Jennifer leaned forward. "I want to learn!"

"That is the last thing we need," Stephen opined, but he leaned back in his chair with a grin.

"*Fine.*" Hsu dropped her hands. "The first thing you have to know is that every facility administrator is crooked. Every one of them," she repeated, for emphasis. "*Maybe* a few of them are crooked in a good way—like that one scientist we met at Istaravshan. Possibly. But that just means they're on a different side from the rest of the organization. Oof. I'm not explaining this well. One second."

She considered, trying to explain what had seemed like basic concepts in China to people here.

"I think I can help," Stoyan offered. "It is not so different in Bulgaria." He sat on the arm of Arisha's chair and looked at Jennifer. "What she means is, every administrator is hiding something. Either they do everything they are told—which, in an organization like Hugo's is against the law and also a terrible thing to do—*or* they are disobeying orders in some way. Sometimes this means they're better than their orders, sometimes it means they're worse."

"*Worse?*" Jennifer demanded.

Stoyan nodded sadly. "It happens. The thing is, either way, Hsu knows, as 'Chief Administrator,'" he made finger quotes, "that she can throw them under the bus and blackmail them, and they know it, too. Every time she walks in, there is a…deal being made. If she asks them to do something wrong—they have leverage on her, but if she makes it clear that she knows what *they* do, then it's back to a stalemate. But as long as she seems to be following Hugo's orders, none of them will fight her too much. They know what Hugo does to people he doesn't like, and they know that she could ruin them if they ever made it out and back to the real world again."

Jennifer frowned, trying to follow this.

"Did that make sense to you?" she demanded of Stephen.

"Yes." Stephen was grinning. "Sometimes you're such a precious, pure little unicorn, you know that?"

"I'll get you for that." Jennifer narrowed her eyes at him. "Maybe not today. Maybe not tomorrow. But I'll get you for that."

Stephen laughed.

"Stephen?" ADAM said.

Everyone in the room perked up. ADAM had used the intercoms on the *ArchAngel*, not an implant.

"Yes?" Stephen asked.

"If you are not going to be murdered, there is a call for you from Emeric Carre."

Arisha hid a laugh behind her hand.

"Thank you, ADAM." Stephen was composed. "I don't think I'm going to die in the next few minutes. I trust Jennifer will let me finish my duties to the Queen before she kills me."

Jennifer shrugged.

"But you'd better put the call through soon," Stephen continued with a grimace. "I don't know how long I've got."

9

QBS *ArchAngel*

"Mr. Carre." Stephen straightened his cuffs as he sat behind the conference table.

ADAM had been able to establish a link to the man's computer, giving them video of him. Tall and burly, with some grey in his hair, he was the spitting image of his father. But where Jean-Marc had looked defeated, Emeric was fiery.

"I'm told you wanted to speak with me," he began abruptly.

"Yes." Stephen inclined his head. "I spoke to a woman named Sidonie, who I gather was acting on your instruction. She asked me to leave the handling of the facilities to you."

That was putting perhaps an excessively cheerful spin on the conversation, but he was determined to begin negotiations pleasantly. Perhaps if they started well, they would not become as unpleasant as his conversation with Sidonie had truly been.

He did not let himself think about what she had said regarding Michael. Such words...

Such words were nothing. Stephen knew that both Michael and Bethany Anne—and likely himself—had accrued enemies despite behaving honorably. Sometimes they had accrued enemies because of it.

He was not going to be swayed by the spiteful words of a woman who only wanted revenge.

He simply did not want to hear such things spoken in his presence again.

Emeric did not seem impressed by Stephen's take on the matter, however. "And you told her you would not step back," he said shortly.

"Yes," Stephen admitted. "That is true."

"Then what do we have to talk about?" Emeric asked him. "Sidonie gave you my demands."

Off-screen, Jennifer bit her lip. She could not begin to think what this must be like for Stephen.

Stephen, however, did not waver, even at the word 'demands.' "Have you given any thought to my offer?" he asked Emeric. "A temporary partnership would be beneficial to both of us."

For one thing, it would provide more manpower. For another, it would show Emeric that Bethany Anne was not someone to defy.

"Partnership." Emeric smiled without even a touch of humor. "A partnership where you would call the shots and I would follow your orders, am I right? That would be no more than us being hired muscle."

"What orders are there to follow?" Stephen asked persuasively. "Both of us want the Wechselbalg in the remaining facilities freed. Both of us want the staff in those facilities to face justice for what they have done."

"Justice. And what does that mean to you?" Emeric sat forward in his seat. "Because let me tell you what would be a just punishment. For a scientist, it would be months in a cage, brought out only to be beaten and tormented, tortured for disobeying the orders to kill their own family —who they would see die before their own eyes, helpless to stop it. For a guard...that is more difficult. Perhaps it would be best if they had to endure all the things they watched and did not stop. And there were many of those."

"And what would you solve?" Stephen asked him. "When you had compounded the horror in your soul twice over by inflicting the same horrors done to you, what would you gain?"

He paused, waiting for a response, but Emeric did not speak.

"There is a reason my Queen forbids torture," Stephen explained. "It accomplishes nothing, and stains those who wield it."

"And so your *Queen* has decided that we are too vengeful to be trusted? That is why she has involved herself in this matter?"

"My Queen," Stephen continued patiently, silently reminding himself that this man had faced unimaginable horrors, "involved herself because she could not sit idly by while Wechselbalg were being abducted and tortured." He knew his voice had risen.

Emeric looked away for a long moment. Stephen did

not know what wheels were spinning in his head, but when he looked up, his face was different.

"I see," he said quietly.

"Do you?" Stephen could not keep the surprise from his voice.

"Yes." This time there was humor in Emeric's voice. "Why do you think I do what I do? Because I cannot stand by. Because I want them freed."

"Exactly." Stephen sighed. "We have stopped the torture —the experiments," he corrected himself. "But we need to end it by clearing out the facilities. We are on the same side, are we not? Should we not work together?"

"Yes, we should." Emeric nodded. "Perhaps we should meet at Naftalan."

"How long until you can be there?" Stephen asked. He did not want to wait very long to free the other facilities.

Emeric considered. "Twelve hours."

They would clear out the other facilities, Stephen decided, then meet him at Naftalan. He would not be pleased, but he should understand that speed was of the essence.

He allowed none of this to show in his face, only nodded. "Twelve hours at the Naftalan facility. One more thing..."

"Yes?"

"Gerard Cordova—"

"The traitor?" Emeric's smile was cold. "Was he ever really a traitor, or was that message from Hugo just you in disguise?"

"Both can be true, can they not?" Stephen smiled. "I sent that message, yes, but he left Hugo to die. You should know, however, that whatever he has offered you—"

"He never got the chance to offer me anything," Emeric interrupted. "He's dead. My pack tore him limb from limb." He spoke the words with grim satisfaction. "I will see you at Naftalan."

He cut the connection and Stephen looked at the others.

"ADAM, show me the trajectory of the plane he's in."

"Of course." ADAM projected it on the far wall.

"You know," Stephen mused, after a pause. "I do believe he's going to try to go to Khachmaz and break the agreement."

"What will we do?" Irina asked.

Stephen's smile was just as grim as Emeric's. "We'll be faster than he is."

A few minutes later, Stephen was alone in the conference room.

"My Queen?"

There was only a slight pause. "Yes?"

"Gerard is dead," Stephen told her without preamble.

"Good. Anything else?"

"All but three of the facilities have now been freed, and the other three will be freed within the next twelve hours. There was a ninth facility in France."

"Which you found."

She was clearly going somewhere with this, though he was too upset to care. "Too late...although the Wechselbalg were all right. They broke themselves out. It appears they took advantage of the confusion my message caused."

"Why do you not seem happy about this?" Bethany Anne asked him.

"We have a situation to resolve." Stephen looked out the window at Earth's glow. "A Wechselbalg named Emeric Carre liberated the facility in France and established himself as Alpha of the 'pack' of prisoners."

"Why do I not like the sound of this?"

"I'm sure you won't have trouble guessing what's happening now," Stephen answered tiredly.

"He wants revenge?"

"Yes." Almost, he had said "bingo"—one of Jennifer's favorite expressions. "I spoke to his father—the original Alpha at Gordes, who set me on the trail. Emeric has agreed to work with us, but it looks as if he'll try to cut us off. He won't be fast enough, of course, but the group that left Gordes has fractured too much for us to find them all in short order...if at all. He claims that this justice is not ours to impose, as we were not the ones tortured."

Bethany Anne did not speak, but her contempt was palpable.

"I do not know if I will be able to reason with him," Stephen said simply.

The question was implied: *What am I authorized to do if he will not listen?*

The answer was quick. "I trust you," Bethany Anne told him. "You've wrapped this up in less than a week. If nothing else, I think this new 'pack' will fracture without leadership. Do what you must."

"He's one of ours," Stephen whispered. "They abducted

him. They made him watch while his family members died. They..."

"And that is why you are going to the facilities." Bethany Anne's voice steadied him. "That is why you are shutting it down. But none of it—none of it—justifies him blowing the lid off the Unknown World and starting a global search for Wechselbalg."

Stephen nodded. Bethany Anne saw to the heart of the matter at once. She always had.

"I will do what I can to persuade him," he offered simply.

"I know you will." He could hear the smile in her voice. "I don't worry about you wantonly killing people."

Stephen managed a laugh at that.

"How's Jennifer?"

"Good. She seems happier after Spain. Sometimes she seems very young, but...never in a bad way. She reminds me to be idealistic."

"What's that like?" She sounded almost wistful.

He chuckled. "And how is Romania?"

"Cold as balls," Bethany Anne replied promptly. "Ecaterina's having the time of her life. We should be wrapped up here in a day or so, and we might be bringing someone back with us. Well, two someones. Believe it or not, Ashur has a crush."

Stephen blinked. "I... Ashur? Really?"

"He found a bitch," Bethany Anne explained, grinning. Ashur must have been there, because he heard her say, "Yes, I was talking about you." She returned to Stephen a moment later. "Her name's Bellatrix. Compared to any other dog, she'd look enormous. They breed German Shepherds big out here."

"And you just *found* her?"

"More or less. Believe it or not, her trainer is here for somewhat the same reason we are. Her brother's been taken by the guys we're after."

"And you think she'll join TQB?" Stephen leaned against the window, feeling himself relax slightly. Soon, he would be back on the ground, facing the horrors of the facilities again. For now, however, he and Bethany Anne could talk about the future—about the organization she was building, and the minutiae of recruitment and the friendships between colleagues.

"I hope so. Ashur will be devastated if she doesn't. The trainer's part Wechselbalg, too."

Stephen whistled. "Oh?"

"Yep. Just enough to communicate with Bellatrix. I get the sense that she's looking for a change of pace. Anyway, you might meet her soon. I'll let you get back to saving the world, shall I?"

Stephen smiled. "Same to you."

Sofia, Bulgaria

Dedov Timurovich stepped off the train and wrinkled his nose. The winter air was crisp, and the afternoon sunshine fell across the cobblestone streets in a pleasant tableau, but he knew the truth of this place.

Bulgaria had been nothing since it broke away.

Hadn't it? He'd read Arisha's article on this place.

He'd read her articles, actually, mostly out of admiration—though he would never admit that. The rest of them sat around, occasionally typing a few lines, waiting for their next assignment. Arisha, though...Arisha always seemed to be going somewhere or doing something. Her articles were always one day early, at least. Usually two days early. And there wasn't much to edit. She hardly ever made mistakes.

She wrote with clarity and passion about the troubles facing former Soviet states. Never enough food, no opportunity. Ruined by America's vision of easy money. They thought they would all have Mercedes and Prada when they broke away, and what did they have now? Nothing.

It...didn't look like they had nothing, though. The people were hurrying to and fro, some stopped at the flower vendors outside the subway stops, some glanced up happily at the buildings and the blue sky.

This was far from the hellish, depressed city he'd expected.

He turned in a slow circle, staring around himself. The article Arisha had written was lies, clearly, but it was just as clear that she had been here—there was the church she had mentioned, and there was the bakery.

So, why had she done it?

The next moment, he cursed himself for a fool. He'd come here precisely *because* he knew Arisha was a liar. When their editor had said, worriedly, that he hadn't heard from Arisha in some days, Dedov had volunteered to go find her—because he'd begun to suspect that she wasn't everything she seemed.

He knew she'd last been in Spain, but he came here first. He was going to be thorough. He would find out what she was hiding.

More than once, he'd left late, only to see Arisha in the records room, poring over old news stories. She shouldn't have had access, and naturally, he feared the worst—but when he later looked over the same articles, he couldn't find any that discussed national security. Nothing even remotely dangerous.

Not only that, she never dated.

Never.

She turned down every offer of a drink politely, but

firmly. She took care with her clothes, but she never preened over her hair or her blouse like other women did. No one ever caught her staring after the women, either, so it clearly wasn't that.

When she didn't come back from Spain on time, Dedov was sure he had stumbled across the truth: Arisha was being paid by someone else to follow much bigger stories than just travel stories. After all, she was always the one to suggest where she went, wasn't she?

She was hiding something big, and he was going to find it. Why shouldn't he have some of the good times, too? Why shouldn't he get to work on this big story? When he found the truth, Arisha would have no choice but to cut him in on the deal, or he'd rat her out.

Dedov smiled to himself and set off for the Hotel Sofia. The trail started there.

QBBS *Meredith Reynolds*

"You wanted to see me?"

Marcus jumped as Barnabas appeared in his peripheral vision. He was *sure* he'd shut the door, and he knew he hadn't heard it open.

Vampires could move far, far too quietly for his liking.

Quick footsteps burst through the door.

"And me," a woman's voice said.

"Tabitha." Barnabas sounded equal parts amused and despairing. "Marcus did not request your presence."

"He *should* have," Tabitha told him confidently. "Whatever he wants your help with, I can help, too!"

Neither man said anything, and her shoulders slumped.

"I'm bored," she admitted.

"Are you not supposed to be training with Ryu?" Barnabas asked her.

"Okay. I'm bored, *and* I don't want a ton of bruises." Her eyes slid to the shining vats pots. "And I kind of hoped you were here to test beer, and I thought I might have some."

"I'm sure that's not why I am here," Barnabas told her patiently.

Marcus decided to interrupt finally. "Actually, it is. Sort of."

Both Tabitha and Barnabas looked at him in surprise.

"Bobcat, William, and I are having a…friendly competition." Marcus stood and came around his desk. He made sure the door was firmly closed and that no one was lurking outside before he spoke again. "I have three beers I am currently planning, all variants on the same, and I hoped to have Barnabas's input on the hops I am using."

Barnabas smiled. "I would be happy to help."

The truth was, he was sometimes nostalgic for his days in the monastery, with the simple rhythms of a monk's life. And he had always enjoyed brewing beer. Like everything, it was a strange mix of precision and art.

He had originally made gruet, a sour beer fermented with an herb mixture. There was a certain peace to be found in pounding and mixing the herbs, but he had also enjoyed the new beers made with hops—ironically, the only type of beer anyone else in the room would recognize. The earthy, sometimes-sharp smell of the hops rose into the air as the beer brewed, becoming at once richer and softer. Flavors deepened and changed. The liquid turned a rich gold.

With so much happening to prepare for the journey through the gate, Barnabas relished the thought of returning to his roots. He smiled at Marcus.

"Which should we look at first?"

"Yeah!" Tabitha was looking at the various copper vats. "Which ones do we get to try?"

"We can't try them yet," Marcus explained. "I haven't even started brewing."

"So...we should come back tonight?"

"The beer will need to ferment for some time," Barnabas informed her. "*Months*," he clarified before she could suggest tomorrow as the time to come back.

"So we don't get to try *anything*?"

"Tell you what." Marcus leaned close. "You should go talk to Bobcat or William, see what they're up to. Ask if they've got anything special you could try. Then you come back and tell me all about it, okay?"

She was gone like a shot.

"EVERY FLAVOR!" Marcus called after her.

"I do not think," Barnabas said carefully, "that she will have an overly-broad lexicon for discussing such flavors."

"Ah." Marcus nodded but then brightened. "Maybe they'll let something slip, though."

He closed the door again, locked it, and brought out three sealed canisters from under his desk. A different arrangement of hops was in each.

He pushed one toward Barnabas, "Now, *this* one was my original concept."

Barnabas opened it and sniffed delicately. "Citrus," he murmured. "Spicy. I like it. Not a boring beer by any measure."

Marcus flushed with pleasure. "Now this one."

Barnabas carefully placed the lid back on the first jar and pulled the second one forward. "Still the citrus, but a more earthy complement. Interesting."

"Do you have a favorite so far?" Marcus asked him.

Barnabas shook his head. "Not yet. What of the third?"

There was a thud outside as Tabitha met the door at high speed, and the sound of inventive cursing made its way through the panel.

"We'll be right out," Marcus called.

He looked back and smiled. Barnabas was breathing in the scent from the third jar with a rapt expression.

"This one," Barnabas said at once. "You should use this one. Citrus, a faint floral taste, the tang of the hops—it will be perfect. Where did you find these hops?"

"Spain, believe it or not." Marcus leaned back in his chair with a smile. "Very good, then. I will begin brewing immediately."

"I must go now, but I would very much like to come back to brew with you," Barnabas said. "It has been a long time."

Marcus smiled. "Welcome to the team, Barnabas. We're going to make some fantastic beer."

And thank you, Bobcat, he thought, with a grin.

Jennifer found Stephen in the medical bay, listening to a list of injuries from one of the techs.

The bay was crowded. Technically, the survivors from Velingrad and Spain would be ready to go home anytime.

Due to the quick healing of those of Wechselbalg blood, and the medical capabilities of the TQB team, their physical injuries were entirely better.

The psychological trauma, however, would take considerably longer.

Stephen looked over as Jennifer approached. He smiled, but there was concern in it.

"Seventy-four percent were treated for hairline fractures," the tech was saying. "A little over half had the lingering effects of repeated concussions, which we think may actually be related to the radio waves. Now, in the children—"

There was a shout from across the lab; someone beckoning the tech.

"I should go attend to that." She looked worried. "I can prepare a full report."

"Yes, please," Stephen told her. "Take your time."

Jennifer drew him away from the crowds. "Are you all right?"

"All right?" He looked confused. "Why would I not be?"

"Because it's hurting you to hear them report the injuries," Jennifer explained bluntly.

"If they could endure the injuries, surely I can endure—"

"You aren't a doctor. You want to have your finger on the pulse of this mission, I get it, but right now you need to be out there doing what you do best—kicking ass and taking names." Jennifer shook her head. "You'll have plenty of time to debrief later. In the meantime, *these* people are as well taken care of as they possibly could be."

"Right." Stephen nodded.

He looked her up and down. Jennifer's boots could match anything from a designer line—Bethany Anne would accept no less for her team—they had more grip than any shoe on the market, and had internal slots for tiny throwing knives and an extra clip for each gun Jennifer carried.

Her leather jacket, retrieved from Velingrad, was similarly kitted out. Stephen could see the lines of the gun harness over her close-fitting shirt.

She grinned and teased him. "Like what you see?"

"Always," Stephen replied emphatically. "Although I was more marveling at the fact that you are always ready to fight."

"You better believe it." Jennifer leaned closer. "Although, when this is all over, I wouldn't mind a nice night out. The taking-down-the-bad-guys dates are fun, I just think maybe we could switch it up a little. Champagne, steaks..."

"I will take you to my favorite restaurant in Paris," Stephen told her.

"Oooh. Wait, is it still around? Because the last one you mentioned closed in eighteen hundred and something."

"It's still around," Stephen assured her with a grin. "I went just last year. Now, let's go finish the facility at Khachmaz and get ready for what I'm assuming will be a fairly unpleasant meeting at Naftalan."

"Fairly unpleasant for *Emeric*, maybe." Jennifer grinned and followed him out of the medical bay.

"You're not at all worried?"

"You eat guys like Emeric for breakfast," Jennifer replied confidently. "I'm just planning to sit back and watch. *Although*...we really should consider letting Hsu have a go."

"About that." Stephen held open a door for her and followed her through. "What would you think of playing the Chief Administrator this time?"

"What, me?" Jennifer started laughing. "I can't act that well!"

"Gotta start somewhere." Stephen grinned. "Besides, the older you get, the more you'll learn that a good con is much better than a fight."

Khachmaz, Azerbaijan

They stepped out of the Pod near Khachmaz in a light dusting of snow.

Arisha was just taking a deep breath of the winter air when she heard a sound she hadn't heard in weeks, the ringing of a cell phone. Bemusedly, she dug it out of her pocket.

"I thought this thing had run out of batteries."

"Wireless charging," Stephen explained. "One of the many, many features of the *ArchAngel*."

"Wow." Arisha looked at the number on the screen and frowned as she accepted the call. "Who is this?"

"Arisha?" The voice was tentative. It continued in Russian. "Is this the right number?"

"*Da*." She realized she'd spoken in English when she picked up. Her English really was getting better, the more she hung around this group.

"It's Kostin."

"Kostin!" Her youngest cousin, and the one who had

been most terrified by the other cousins' stories of the big wolf in the woods so many years ago, Kostin had since grown up to become an engineer. Now he worked at the University of Moscow and was getting married in the spring. "Is this a new phone?"

"*Nyet*, I am calling from work." His voice dropped several notches. "A man came by yesterday. Asking about you."

"About me?" Arisha laughed. "Why?"

"He...said you had gone missing."

"Oh, no. I swear—"

"Well, your mother said she had heard from you a few days back, and all was well, so I did not worry. But then today I called you at your work, and you were not there, and they said that he had gone to look for you."

"Oh..." Arisha squeezed her eyes shut. "Oh, no. Who was it?"

"He said his name was Dedov."

"*Dedov*?" Her voice rose several notches.

Everyone turned to look at her, and she waved them off with a shake of her head and a flap of her hand.

Of all of her coworkers, Dedov had to be one of her least favorite. The man had no real ambition and seemed to believe that he should be granted riches and fame simply for existing. He always moaned about a lack of opportunity, saying there was no way for anyone of their generation to get ahead.

He wanted things, but he didn't want to work for them.

"Where did he go?" Arisha asked quietly.

"I don't know. He said you'd been in Spain, but then he kept mentioning Bulgaria. He kept asking me all of these things I didn't understand like I should know everything about your work. He asked if you ever talked about your 'real' job. Arisha, what do you do for your real job? Are you not a reporter?"

"I'm a reporter." Arisha could not make head nor tail of this. "I don't understand what he's talking about."

"Neither do I, then. I'd say he had the wrong person, but if he found me..." She could practically see Kostin shrug, the way he had started doing when he was fifteen, lanky, and sullen. The gesture was even more endearing in an adult. "I'd talk to him, anyway. He seems to think you found some big story and you're using the newspaper as a cover."

Arisha's blood turned to ice. *Some big story.*

Like werewolves. And if Dedov did, by some twist of fate, manage to stumble onto the story in Bulgaria, she knew exactly what he would do with it—sell it to the highest bidder.

"I have to go, okay? Thanks for calling." She hung up without waiting for an answer and met Stephen's eyes. "I have a problem."

11

___

Khachmaz, Azerbaijan

"What is it, Arisha?" Stephen was worried. He looked at the facility.

Arisha realized he thought something was wrong with the mission—and that she was being foolish.

"No. Not at all. Just something I need to resolve when we're done. I'll need to go to Sofia."

Stoyan was at her side instantly, "What is wrong? What has happened?"

Stephen tilted his head. He also wanted to know what had made Arisha go white as a sheet. The woman was, by and large, unflappable.

"One of my colleagues, Dedov…he has been tracing my steps over the past few articles. He thinks I have found a big story and am using my work as a travel reporter to cover my movements." Arisha hung her head. "The funny thing is, it's true." She gave a humorless laugh.

"You're worried he'll expose you?" Irina asked.

"No. I can get a new job if I need to. I am worried he will learn what happened in that facility. Dedov is always looking for a way to get rich quickly. He would sell the information to anyone who would buy it, and then you'd have companies and *countries* descending on Bulgaria, searching out Wechselbalg. I can't let him find what he's after, but he can always sniff out a lie."

"Maybe you tell him the truth about where Emeric Carre is, and the problem will solve itself," Jennifer murmured.

Stephen tried not to laugh. "We will, of course, take care of this soon."

"Yes. Thank you." Arisha nodded down the hill, to where the factory poked out of the snow-covered ground. "This is more urgent. I just panicked."

"After what Filip did, selling us out to Hugo, I'm not surprised," Stephen told her.

Stoyan growled softly. Part of him still could not believe that Filip was dead. He could hardly believe how much damage a selfish person could cause. Filip, blinded by his own self-interest, had nearly caused the deaths of hundreds.

He would not let anyone do the same again.

He leaned close to Arisha as they descended the hill toward the factory. "I will come with you to Bulgaria to deal with this Dedov."

Arisha smiled at Stoyan, "Thank you. Although…if he is following the trail of what I found, is it wise for you to be around?"

"I hadn't thought of that." Stoyan frowned. "What if—"

They reached the gate, and he broke off as Jennifer

swiped her access badge and the gates started to slide open with a screech.

Guards poured out of the building as the gates opened, running for the gate with their guns half-raised and yelling for the intruders to halt. Jennifer and the rest stood patiently until they arrived.

"Hello," Jennifer began pleasantly when they stopped moving. "I need to speak to the administrator, please."

The guards exchanged a look. This was not, after all, how break-ins were expected to go.

"Immediately," Jennifer continued, trying to sound bored. "If you would."

"I, uh..." One of the guards toward the back straightened up. "I'll go tell him. Who should I say you are?"

"Chief Administrator Zhang," Jennifer informed him.

There was a long pause while Stephen refrained from dropping his face into his hands and Hsu tried not to let her mouth twitch.

"*Not* to be confused with Associate Administrator Zhang," Jennifer recovered. She pointed imperiously at Hsu.

The guard blinked at her for a moment, and then hurried back over the cold ground.

Jennifer waited, arms crossed.

She was pleased to see the administrator hurry out a few minutes later, accompanied by some of the senior scientists. The man bobbed his head nervously.

"We were informed that you would be arriving, Chief Administrator. What do you need from us to begin the shutdown of the facilities?"

"Only for the scientists to withdraw outside the walls."

Jennifer gestured to Arisha and Stoyan. "My associates will direct you to the correct place to wait for pickup. In the meantime, we will begin *dealing with* the experiments." She allowed her smile to slip a little, a clear indication of what the phrase meant.

"Of course, of course. A regrettable necessity." The administrator bobbed his head again. "And will the scientists be able to return to the facility to collect their things after you've...well...?" His voice trailed off, and he looked at Jennifer hopefully.

Never had she wanted so badly to punch someone in the face.

"Of course," Jennifer managed, with a smile. "You might have to wait for some time for the gas to clear, but this should be handled immediately.

She waited as the man gave the order, and then scientists and guards began to stream out of the buildings. All of them nodded politely to the party at the gates, and a few could be overheard speaking about the inconvenience of wasting their time on a dead-end project.

Jennifer struggled to keep her face flat. It wasn't lying that was the hard part of pulling a con, she realized. It was trying not to let your emotions get the better of you. She wanted to terrify every one of these people, make them beg for their lives—and make very sure they knew that they had no right to ask forgiveness.

She stayed composed until the building was confirmed empty by ADAM, and then she strode across the icy ground to free her brethren, while Stephen lingered behind with the doomed staff.

Naryn, Kyrgyzstan

"Are you sure our information was good?" Ruslan peered out from behind the trees at the gate of the facility.

For months, they had tried to find a way into this place with no luck. The guards did not ever go to the bars in town or frequent the prostitutes, and the facility was owned by a set of shell corporations that were layered too deep to find the true owners.

But they didn't need to know things like that to know what went on inside. The evening breeze often carried screams, and personnel in white lab coats could be seen on the grounds.

There was just no way to get *in*.

"Do we have any choice?" Aibek muttered back. "We have to do what we can now."

Last night, they had been contacted—through a liaison —by a woman named Sidonie. She had transformed to show her powers, then in halting English, explained that the facilities were being closed down. How she knew this, she did not say.

But she knew, also, that the facilities were waiting for personnel to come—and that if the Aibek's pack conned their way in now, they would be able to get their family out early.

"What do we do with the scientists?" Aibek had asked her.

She smiled coldly. "Whatever you wish."

"And what do you want in return for this information?" Ruslan had asked her.

He was always the sensible one, Ruslan. Always the cold one. A good second in command, though Aibek couldn't care less what the woman wanted. Anything he had was hers. He would give anything to have his family back.

Sidonie, however, did not seem offended by the question.

"Your help. This is not the only facility, and there are many, all across Europe, who have aided these torturers. My alpha, Emeric Carre, would like your help to defeat them."

Aibek had looked at Ruslan, who had nodded without hesitation.

Wherever there were people doing things like this, they would do their utmost to free the captives and destroy the captors.

"Deal," Aibek agreed.

"Good. Get your family out of the facility, then contact me, and I will tell you where to go."

So here they were, slinking over the ground in borrowed suits.

Tell them we are the team to shut down the facility. Aibek went over the plan in his head. *Tell them that they are to leave the building immediately and wait outside. Whatever they ask, about payment or anything else, promise them what they want. When the pack is free...kill them.*

Could he pull it off?

He had to.

They stood in front of the gates and pressed the buzzer.

"Yes?" The voice that came from the box was distorted, but clearly bored.

"We have been sent to close down this facility," Aibek announced. "Please open the gates."

"What are your names?"

"Administrators Beshimov and Nogoyev." Aibek's heart was pounding in his chest.

"And how do we check your credentials?"

Aibek froze.

"However you wish," Ruslan snapped rudely. "Are you asking me how to do your job?"

Aibek looked at him sharply, and Ruslan shrugged. *Just trying something,* his gaze said.

"I...of course not." The voice seemed flustered. "One moment, please."

Ruslan and Aibek waited, arms crossed, trying not to pace.

However, a moment later, the gates swung open. Both men walked tentatively into the open space of the courtyard, trying not to look around. The ground was barely thawing now, but there were no shoots of green grass underfoot.

What *was* this place? Aibek was afraid of what he would find.

At the door, a guard held the door open for them. He ushered them into the warmth of the building and led them to a small room with two chairs and a table.

"You are to wait here," he informed them. His tone was deferential, even embarrassed. "We would offer you tea, but we have not received supplies in days. Our apologies. We will send the rest of the team to join you when they arrive."

He left before either Aibek or Ruslan could say anything.

But as soon as he was gone, Aibek looked at Ruslan, his heart sinking.

"The rest of the team?"

Khachmaz, Azerbaijan

Stephen had just stepped away from the bodies of the scientists when ADAM's voice sounded in his earpiece.

"Two individuals are trying to gain access to the facility at Naryn."

Stephen froze. How could anyone from Emeric's team have gotten there so quickly?

"Do you know anything about them?"

"No. The facility is requesting authorization from Hugo, checking that they are the correct people to let in. It appears that they do not have badges or any other gear."

Stephen considered this. It appeared that Emeric had decided to take matters entirely into his own hands. They would need to evacuate Naryn and Naftalan immediately after Khachmaz.

"What did you tell the facility?" he asked finally.

"That I was researching their credentials."

"Good thinking. Tell them that the two are authorized, but that they should wait for the rest of the team."

No gear, no badges, and no backup. It was likely that these infiltrators had no experience in this and would be easily unbalanced by the first sign of trouble.

"Would I be correct in thinking that you wish to join them there?"

"That's exactly what I'm planning, yes," Stephen told the AI.

He jerked his head to Arisha and Stoyan to follow him back up the hill, where a Pod descended to wait for them.

"ADAM, patch me through to Jennifer for a moment?"

"You're live."

"Jennifer, I need to go to the Naryn facility. I think two of Emeric's men are there, but they seem to be alone. I'm taking Arisha and Stoyan."

"Okay." Jennifer's voice filtered back. "We'll finish up here and…meet you there?"

"No, go straight to Naftalan. Emeric is trying to head us off. We can't let him, or this whole thing is going to blow up," Stephen said grimly. "I don't trust that man's sense of revenge."

"Right." She was quiet for a moment. "Be safe."

"You as well."

He cut the connection and stepped into the Pod.

The journey to Naryn was short, hardly a few long breaths of time before the door slid open again on a new tableau.

It didn't feel as if the Pod had moved, and Stephen experienced a sense of dislocation. It was still odd to him to travel so fast.

Naryn, Kyrgyzstan

He strode through the trees to the gates and was met by a guard who smiled at him.

"Come with me," the guard told him, sounding relieved that everything was falling into place. "The administrators are waiting."

"Thank you," Stephen replied calmly.

They followed the guard through the corridors until

they stopped at a closed door. The guard opened it and waited as Stephen ducked inside.

"You may go for now," Stephen said. "We will need to speak to your administrator, but we will come to the office when we are finished discussing closedown procedure with our colleagues."

"Of course, sir." The guard half-bowed and withdrew.

Stephen turned to the two men who were staring at him in anger and fear.

"So," he asked calmly, "who are you?"

12

Khachmaz, Azerbaijan

Jennifer emerged into the weak afternoon sunlight.

A group of three scientists trailed her nervously. They had been found trying to disable the poison mechanisms, and one had thrown himself in front of the other two, trying to sacrifice himself so that they could finish their sabotage and save the Wechselbalg.

Jennifer had been impressed despite herself. The scientists at the other facilities worked alone if they even rebelled, but these three had been brave enough to seek each other out and make a plan. Apparently, they had even told the captive Wechselbalg that they would get them out as soon as the evacuation started.

When Jennifer explained who she was and why she was there—along with the truth of the message from "Hugo"—they had broken down in tears. Like Hsu, they seemed to believe that they could never make up for what they had done while in the facility.

But, as with Hsu, she wasn't willing to give up on them yet.

She nodded to Hsu, and her companion led the scientists to a Pod for just the four of them. It ascended, disappearing into the sky, and Jennifer looked around to locate Irina.

The woman was moving confidently and quickly, as she always did these days. She ushered groups of Wechselbalg into the Pods as they traveled back and forth from the *ArchAngel*. There were only a few more trips to go, and Jennifer settled down on a nearby bench to watch.

Irina had a natural air of command about her now, but Jennifer knew it was not the type of command to clash with an Alpha. Irina would never stand against Nathan, for instance. It was simply that, right now, she knew what had to be done and she did it without any hesitation.

She also knew that type of authority was one of the best things for people who were shell-shocked. What the Wechselbalg here needed, after months of pain and uncertainty, was someone to assure them that all would be well and that they would get the care they needed. Once their wounds had been treated and the initial surge of adrenaline had worn off, they would feel much better.

"ADAM, is everything okay with space on the *ArchAngel*?"

"Yes," ADAM responded at once. "The evacuees from Velingrad have been able to return to their homes, by and large, with Sergio as our emissary to the local pack leaders. They will contact us if Emeric tries to turn them to his cause. And the captives from Spain have been transferred to one of our buildings in the U.S. We will return them shortly, but the entire town is in chaos now that Hugo is dead, and Lance decided it was better to keep them out of that. We now have room for new evacuees."

"Excellent," Jennifer told him.

She had a suspicion that Sergio might soon be an Alpha in one of the packs near Velingrad. The man's resilience was incredible, and his kindness when dealing with the evacuees had been noteworthy. They had left him behind on the *ArchAngel*, because although he made a powerful fighter, he provided much comfort to the other Wechselbalg.

Jennifer hoped he would consider joining Bethany Anne's team, but she knew that, like many in the Unknown World, he might choose to stay on the planet he knew.

She couldn't blame him for that.

She heard her name and saw Irina waving at her.

"The last of them are off to the *ArchAngel*," Irina reported. "And you said we're to go to Naftalan after this?"

"Yes. If Hsu can come back with a Pod, we'll go with her. It's too bad we don't have a bigger team, but we also don't have time to wait."

It was clear that Emeric did not have the first idea what he was up against.

Well, that was his problem.

They waited while Hsu came back and stepped into the Pod together. This would be a very short journey.

Hsu turned to Jennifer, "The scientists have offered to testify."

Jennifer snorted. She had little faith that the whole network of minor officials and bureaucrats would ever be brought to justice. Hugo had not created the corruption or lack of honor in the world, he had merely exploited it.

Hsu looked sad at her response, so Jennifer caught her eye again and smiled.

"It's good of them to offer. I'm sure they'll be able to help us somehow."

Hsu smiled eagerly at that. "They want to," she assured Jennifer. "And they had a good plan. I think they could have pulled it off." Her face fell. "I didn't have the heart to tell them what happened to the others."

Jennifer looked away.

It was hard for people from the human world to understand the justice of the Unknown World. They weren't used to being judged by both their actions and the content of their character. For Hsu and the scientists who had just been rescued, their colleagues' execution likely felt abrupt —and like something they had only narrowly escaped.

Jennifer tried not to shake her head. Humans were odd, that was all there was to it. Maybe Ecaterina could shine some light on the subject when next they met.

In the meantime, they had work to do. The Pod door slid open, and Jennifer flashed Irina and Hsu a smile.

"Let's go finish this."

Naryn, Kyrgyzstan

"Who are we?" Aibek raised an eyebrow. "Who are *you*?"

"No. You first." Stephen pulled out one of the chairs and sat, unbuttoning his jacket. He looked the two of them up and down. Neither responded.

The one who had spoken first was likely the ranking

member of the pack, but the second would be the one who thought all of this was a mistake, who was likely far more cautious than his pack leader. He was the one who watched the pack leader's back and provided protection.

Not the weaker link, then.

Stephen returned his attention to the first speaker, "Some weeks ago, my organization became aware of a number of facilities across Europe. Since that time, we have destroyed all but two of them, released the Wechselbalg who were held captive and offered them medical treatment, and we have taken down the man at the center of all of this. Our...programmers...are the reason that this facility's request for authorization came to us, rather than someone who might have ordered you both killed outright."

"Programmers?"

"I don't have the time to explain to you right now," Stephen subvocalized. "Maybe later."

Both men looked uncomfortable, but neither of them had spoken.

Stephen locked onto the first man's eyes. "And then, a couple of days ago, one of the facilities was freed by a man named Emeric Carre."

Both of them twitched at the sound of that name.

Gott Verdammt.

"Mr. Carre has ideas that he will get revenge for what happened at these facilities," Stephen told them. "Doubtless it is a seductive thought, but it is also foolish because Mr. Carre does not want to stop his revenge at those who were in the facilities and any others who knew. He wants to take revenge on all of human society."

The two Wechselbalg looked uncertain now.

"Your pack has been taken from you," Stephen told them. "I will not lie to you, the truth of what has been done to them is terrible. And I will help you free them, and make sure that they are well. But you and I both know that exposing the Unknown World to humanity at large is no kind of solution."

The men looked at one another.

"So, I will ask one last time. Who are you, and why are you here?"

There was a pause, and the first man bowed his head in defeat. He took the seat across from Stephen. "Aibek Beshimov. This is Ruslan Nogoyev. As you say, we were contacted by Emeric Carre. He told us that the facilities were waiting to be closed down and that if we pretended to be the ones sent to do it, we could likely get our families out before reinforcements arrived. And..." He swallowed. "He said we could do whatever we wanted to the staff here."

"Doubtless that was a seductive thought," Stephen replied. He could admit that much. "Did you not think, however, that a man who—"

"No." Aibek interrupted him with a shake of his head.

Stoyan growled, deep in his throat. *You speak out of turn.*

"I didn't think. I didn't care." Aibek was shaking. "I had been trying to get to them for months, and I was desperate. I would have sold my soul to the devil to get them back, do you understand me? I didn't know *you* were coming. I was offered a way in, and I took it."

Stephen paused.

"I can understand that," he agreed finally. He bowed his head for a moment. "And now?"

"Now, I..." Aibek squeezed his eyes shut. "I still want to hurt them," he confessed. "And all I can think of is my family upstairs. What did they do to them here?"

"They wanted an obedient army of Wechselbalg," Stephen explained simply. "They tried to force a shift, and to give orders to the wolves. Sometimes, though rarely, they were successful."

Aibek and Ruslan looked at one another, worriedly.

"The rest, they will tell you themselves if they wish." Stephen spoke quietly but adamantly. "I can promise you that those who participated willingly in this—those who did nothing to stop it—will see no clemency."

The two shifters considered.

"Will you join us?" Stephen asked.

There was no hesitation in either man. They nodded.

"We need your help," Aibek admitted.

"And we do not want to be allied with a madman," Ruslan added.

Ruslan would not have admitted as much to Aibek, but he was relieved. He had not liked the subtle suggestion of debt that Sidonie had made—that their pack would always be indebted to Emeric Carre. It was true, but to remind them of it suggested that they would be asked to go above and beyond any reasonable call of loyalty.

Whatever Emeric had been planning to ask of them, Ruslan had been quite sure that he wanted no part of it.

But, like Aibek, he had seen no recourse.

Now they had a new ally.

"What of our promise to Emeric?" Ruslan asked quietly.

"I will deal with Emeric," Stephen assured them. "But first, let us find your family and get them out."

Sofia, Bulgaria

By early afternoon, Dedov was annoyed, and still no closer to finding anything about Arisha.

He had started at the hotel. Aside from some gossip amongst the bell boys about several abrupt departures from the highest-end suites in the place, there didn't seem to be much information to be had. The woman at the front desk refused to confirm whether Arisha had even stayed in the hotel, citing confidentiality rules, and though she was clearly there to serve as eye candy, both her tone and her manner said that she was intended for higher-end people than him.

In the end, she reverted to Bulgarian instead of Russian or English, and he was forced to withdraw to the bar, sulking.

He wandered through a few streets and markets, asking after his friend who had "disappeared from home." He got a few sympathetic looks, but no one seemed to have seen her. Once or twice, he thought he might have been being followed, but when he looked around, no one was there.

Finally, he had an idea.

He strolled around, looking in the windows of the bars until he found one that seemed to be a good mix of completely run-down and almost empty.

A few old men were playing darts in the corner, slurring their words. Another two men argued around the far corner of the bar. They slapped the bar regularly for emphasis.

The seats were disgusting, but Dedov sat on one of them anyway and caught the bartender's attention with a lift of his chin.

"Vodka," he ordered simply. He waited for the pour and wrinkled his nose. The generosity of it suggested that the vodka wasn't very good.

However, he had been raised properly. He drank the first vodka down and asked for another, trying not to wince at the unusual burn in the back of his throat. What was this stuff made of?

He drank the second one down, too—to show that the first was not bad—and asked for a third. This one, he cradled in one hand and took a tiny sip.

"I'm looking for something," he told the bartender.

"Ah?" The bartender gave a leisurely look around the bar as if checking on his patrons and then leaned in to wipe down the bar near Dedov. "Drugs? A girl?...A boy?"

Dedov shook his head. "No, nothing so...nothing like that." He took another sip of the vodka and kept himself from wincing. "Information. Anything strange that has been occurring lately."

The bartender looked wary. "I'm sure I don't know anything." He forced a smile. "Tell me if you need another drink."

He vanished, and Dedov cursed under his breath.

A voice spoke from behind him. "I could tell you some strange things."

Dedov turned sharply. A man stood there, with pale eyes and light brown hair. His soccer jersey was familiar—

NATALIE GREY & MICHAEL ANDERLE

Dedov had seen him earlier in the day. Now that he thought of it, he had seen the man more than once.

"Were you following me?"

"I heard someone was asking questions." The man took a seat beside him and raised two fingers to the bartender to indicate two more drinks.

They did not speak until the bartender had brought the drinks back, and then disappeared with almost unseemly haste.

"You see..." The man clinked his glass against Dedov's and took a long pull of his beer. "I have also been asking questions. And I have heard some answers that mention a woman. A Russian woman who was here not too long ago, asking questions of her own."

"Arisha?" Dedov asked sharply.

"Yes. Your friend, then?"

"Coworker." Dedov took a gulp of his drink. "We're reporters, and she found something big. I don't know what, but I'm not going to let her take the payout and run. I want in."

"Interesting." The man took a sip of his beer.

"What were you asking questions about?" Dedov asked.

"My friend. He worked as a...connector." The man shrugged. "He found people whatever they wanted, *da*? He went missing from here not too long ago, and I wanted to find him. Not long before he died, he called in some guys he'd used as muscle once or twice before. He said he had some information that would impress a girl. He was seen once more, coming out of a building on the night of the bombing—and then never again."

"Bombing?" Dedov's eyes widened.

"Ah, yes. Some very strange things have been happening lately." The man smiled. "We could find the truth together, you and I."

"Deal." Dedov held out his hand. "I'm Dedov."

"Milen." The man shook his hand and drank down his beer. "Now, come with me."

Dedov left some money on the bar and followed the man out into the fresh air.

"What did you say your friend's name was?" he asked, as they walked.

"Filip," Milen told him.

Naftalan, Azerbaijan

The facility near Naftalan was shielded not by trees but by mountains. It lay nestled in a valley, relatively far from the city. Boulders littered the area, and Jennifer's boots crunched as she climbed up the steep incline with Irina and Hsu following her.

On the one hand, they would have the high ground as they approached the facility. On the other hand, they would be entirely exposed, with only bushes and rocks as occasional cover.

If the guards at Naftalan decided to shoot first and ask questions later, there was going to be a problem.

They were most of the way up the hill that led into the valley when the wind shifted and Irina and Jennifer caught the scent of another Wechselbalg.

Their heads whipped around as the sound of growls filled the air, and a giant, silvery wolf slunk out from behind one of the boulders. There was no way it couldn't know what they were, but it also did not look friendly in the least.

Possibilities whirled in Jennifer's head. Had the administrator of the Naftalan facility sent wolves out here with orders?

That would mean their experiments had been successful, allowing for implanted orders without any further radio waves—for she did not sense any. And she was fairly sure that none of the facilities had been successful in their efforts.

So who was this?

"We do not mean to trespass." Jennifer held up her hands and nodded to the wolf. "We are here to free the inhabitants of the facility."

Mentally, she prepared herself to transform and leap in front of Hsu. It was clear that the human was the weakest target of all of them, and the wolf would no doubt go there first.

The wolf transformed back into a woman. It was difficult to tell her age—anywhere between forty and sixty would be Jennifer's guess. Her grey-and-white hair fell over her shoulders, and though her face was relatively unlined, her eyes were watchful and wise.

And unfriendly. Her face never cracked a smile as she retrieved some clothes and put them on. She crossed her arms and stared them down.

"You're with the vampire," she said bluntly.

"The Matriarch?" Jennifer deliberately misunderstood.

"Or her servant. You reek of it." The woman's nose twitched in distaste. "We heard you would come here and tell us how to seek justice."

"So says Emeric Carre, who would bring the attention of the world down on you with no way to protect you from it," Jennifer spoke flatly. "He cannot be trusted. He is not your friend. He has been driven mad by his need for revenge."

"The fact that you are *not* mad for revenge means *you* are not trustworthy." The woman glared. "Do you not understand what has happened here?"

"I understand it," Jennifer countered heatedly.

"And I have lived it," Irina chimed in. "But I do not seek to wander into towns and murder humans for the crime of not knowing that I was tortured. They did not even realize that I existed, and if you cannot save your kin, as my kin could not save me...how should the humans have saved us?"

The woman wavered at that, but fury snapped back onto her face a moment later.

"Do not try to trick me out of having my revenge. Every one of the humans in that facility deserves to die—followed by every human who knew of it and did nothing to stop it."

The sound of a rock clinking caught Jennifer's attention, and she looked around and saw the rest of the pack emerging from the rocks some distance away. They walked up the hill toward her, forming a loose net to catch her and her companions.

Nowhere to run—except the facility, itself.

But Jennifer smiled. The woman was counting on her to back down, perhaps to be cowed into submission so she could be brought to Emeric. And that wasn't going to happen.

She waited until the pack was close enough to hear her, and then she struck. "So, you want to make sure that everyone involved in this is dead, and you do not trust me and mine to do that?"

The woman looked briefly surprised that Jennifer was not backing down, but she nodded. "Yes."

"What is your name?" Jennifer asked.

The woman glowered, then, "Zurya."

"Zurya, do you know who runs these facilities?" Jennifer asked, tilting her head toward the lab.

"No one knows."

"I know." Jennifer smiled. "His name is Hugo Marcari. Or…it was. I killed him."

There was a sharp intake of breath around the group, and a murmur started. Everyone quieted when the woman gave a look of warning.

"A person and a claim we cannot verify," Zurya pointed out.

"Then how on earth do you expect to find out in the first place?" Jennifer asked her, raising an eyebrow. "If you admit that you have no way to find out if I'm telling the truth—which, by the way, I am—then you're as good as admitting that you'll never find out who's behind all of this."

"Get off our land," Zurya spat.

"No," Jennifer said flatly. "We have an AI hooked into the computer systems of that facility. We have access to badges. We have ways to shut down the automated systems that would kill the prisoners if the facility was stormed and someone pressed a panic button. We have the medical facilities to treat the Wechselbalg in there, and we have enough firepower to take out every single scientist and guard in that place. We know all of this because we did our research. We found out who was behind this and we hacked their system to find every facility.

"But you don't have any of that. You're going to try to get in there unarmed, talking your way into a situation you've never seen before, and you're going to try to get in and out without knowing what sort of defensive systems there are in place or how many guards there are. Explain to me why I should leave. I'm the one who's going to save the people in there—and you're the one who's going to get them killed if you don't work with me."

There was a stony silence. Then—

"Are you challenging me?" Zurya demanded.

Fury filled Jennifer's chest. Lives were at stake, and all this woman cared about was rank.

"Yes," she told her curtly. "If I win, I will be the one who takes charge of this assault. Are we clear? And when this is all done, I will leave all of you here. I will have no more orders. And you can try to become alpha again." She felt compelled to add. "I don't like your chances, though."

"If I win," the woman replied quietly, "you will leave and not interfere in something that is none of your business."

So, not a fight to the death, then. It was all Jennifer could think.

Despite her words, despite the traditional use of "if," she did not even think of what would happen if she lost. She could not afford failure. Therefore, she would not fail.

They shed their clothes without another word, and Irina drew Hsu away to the edge of the circle that had formed. When Jennifer and the alpha transformed and began to circle, there was a quiet murmur.

Jennifer had always been a strong fighter. It had been both a blessing and a curse, condemning her to difficult jobs as a lowly member of the pack and tending to make the men afraid of her.

She curled her lip in amusement at the thought of what those men would think now. She had been a strong fighter, yes, but she had never truly been tried in battle. She had never gone up against Nathan or Pete. She had never known what it was to really *fight* with everything she had.

Over months of fighting and having the rest of Bethany Anne's team absolutely wipe the floor with her, she became stronger. She'd gotten quicker, and she'd learned to push past the point of exhaustion. She'd determined that neither enhancements nor technology was a substitute for tactics and practice.

Now, as Zurya leaped, Jennifer's body moved without thought. She leaped uphill and out of the way. It was a harder move, something that cost strength and stamina— not something she would have spent her energy on at the beginning of the fight.

Now she knew that when the dust settled, she would have the high ground, and Zurya would be easily pinned against one of the boulders.

Even as she landed, Jennifer was turning to leap again. Her jaws found the other wolf's scruff as the alpha tried to turn, and Jennifer slammed her opponent into the rock with a snarl.

End the fight now, decisively, or prove over a longer period of time that she was the true victor and not just the recipient of a lucky break? Jaws still locked on, Jennifer dragged Zurya into the circle, pinning her until she yipped in defeat.

Jennifer changed back and donned her clothes, looking away courteously until the other woman was also dressed.

When she turned back, however, she did not pull any punches. "I didn't come here to get mixed up in your pack. I came here to save your families. If you want to help me, you're welcome to—although there will not be any torture. This time spent positioning for power was additional time your families remain inside.

"So do you want to help me, or do you want to stand in the way?"

Zurya did not look at her. "I will help."

"Good." Jennifer nodded. "Now, here's the deal. Each facility so far, we've had our AI intercept communications and give authorization that we're the team being sent to close down the facility. So far, there hasn't been much trouble. But things might go sideways. *If they do...* Go to the second and third floors of the facility and get your family members out. My team can shut down any poison or other defensive systems, and Irina and I will handle taking out the guards. So far, none of them have had silver bullets."

"There's something, at least," Zurya murmured.

"Yes." Jennifer allowed herself a small smile. "So let's get in there and see what we can make happen."

Sofia, Bulgaria

Dedov followed Milen through the underbrush,

swearing as branches flicked back to slap him across the face.

Milen looked back, half amused and half annoyed. "Be quieter."

"You didn't tell me we were going to be going to the middle of nowhere," Dedov complained. "What's out here that we can't find out about in the city?"

"The bombed facility," Milen called over his shoulder. "Stop complaining."

As soon as they had left the bar, Milen had led Dedov to a run-down shop at the edge of town with surprisingly durable cold weather gear. A few words, a discreet handshake, and they'd been on their way out into the forests outside the town.

But the cold got in any way. It seeped into the boots and lashed against their faces, and Dedov was slowly getting more and more annoyed.

Wasn't this the sort of thing you hired other people to do, instead of doing it yourself?

"What's at the facility?" He called, after a few more minutes of struggling across snow and tripping over hidden branches.

Milen sighed and turned. "We don't *know*," he explained patiently. "If we knew, we wouldn't have to come out. But I know your precious Arisha was asking questions about wolves, and I know wolf howls were heard around here, and I know Filip was trying to get answers out of some American to give to Arisha, *and* I know that the *American* was interested in this place. Are you done with the questions?"

Dedov stared at him. His head was spinning from the

influx of information. It was all tangled up, but damned if he could see how it all fit together.

As he followed Milen, his head began to churn. He had read over every folder he'd seen Arisha sneaking peeks at, and although he'd never found anything like secret government activity or bribery scandals, he had seen a few articles about wolf sightings.

Now he tried to remember everything he could.

Why the hell was Arisha so interested in wolves? Wolves were a nuisance, nothing more—certainly, it wasn't worth traveling to find stories about wolves in other countries.

Was it?

But suddenly, Dedov remembered something from one of the articles and his blood ran cold.

It had been one of those stories that showed up in tabloids or local news. A farmer had seen a wolf, but not just *any* wolf—a wolf he claimed was as tall at its crest as a man's shoulder, silhouetted against the moon.

It was too fantastical a story to be believed, but the farmer had not been drunk and, even after being laughed out of the police station and off the television, he stuck stubbornly to his story. *I saw it,* Dedov remembered reading. *I saw it, and I'm not going to say I didn't. I don't know how it's real—it just is.*

Now he swallowed with fear, suddenly terrified.

What if the wolf *had* been real?

He pushed himself as fast as he could until he came up alongside his companion.

"She's been looking into wolves for a while," he confided. "The sort of stories you hear from your grandma when you're little, and she's trying to scare you—people saying they saw giant wolves."

Milen stilled. "Giant wolves? And you're sure your friend came here looking for that?"

"I'm not sure," Dedov replied. "But I know she was reading about it back in Moscow, and if you said she was asking about wolves here..." He shrugged, then caught sight of the man's expression. "What is it?"

"There were sightings of a giant wolf around here some weeks ago," Milen told him. "I didn't think anything of it. I didn't even connect it to this. We have wolves, but what they do is make off with sheep and kill cows. I guess I just never thought someone would actually be..." He shook his head. "Be on your guard," he suggested finally. "Nothing should be alive up here anymore, but better safe than sorry."

Naryn, Kyrgyzstan

Stephen climbed the stairs to the administrator's office, Aibek at one shoulder and Arisha at the other. Stoyan and Ruslan hung back, both accustomed to being The Muscle in any operation.

It was a deliberate choice. The guards at this facility, like the ones at the other facilities, might have been hired in top physical condition, but they certainly weren't there any longer. Months without access to the outside world, locked into a dull, unrelenting schedule and deprived of any meaningful training had made these guards both weak and weary.

By having Stoyan and Ruslan walk behind him, Stephen showed the staff of the Naryn facility that he was more qualified to deal with the wolves. The mere sight of his guards reminded them of how frightened they were of their captives.

And none of them realized how dangerous Stephen was, himself. The thought made him smile.

The administrator's door stood open, and the scent of fresh-brewed coffee made its way down the hall. The administrator had clearly been told to expect Stephen's group.

When they appeared, the man wore a desperate, pained smile.

"We're so glad to have you here," he began, without preamble. "When we heard the facilities were being shut down..." His throat worked.

"Yes?" Stephen took a seat without being asked. He was raging with impatience to get this over with, but the appearance of hurry often tripped people's internal alarm bells.

"Let me simply say, I had no wish to disappoint Mr. Marcari," the administrator explained carefully. "It was to my abiding regret that I was not able to produce the results he wished to see. I admit that I was relieved to know that I had not been the only one to fail."

It was an impressive speech only because it was so unusual. The administrator did not blame his staff, and he did not shy away from the blunt truth of his failure. But Stephen also knew what lengths these facilities would go to try to achieve the results Hugo sought.

"You used a range of techniques, I would guess," he suggested blandly.

"Yes." The administrator pulled out a stack of folders. "In the end, the most persuasive techniques were not those that were used at the moment, but over time. The... subjects...are very proud, you see. They do not like to take orders. We had to break them of that. Well, we had to try. Regrettably, we did not succeed."

"Most regrettable." His sympathy entirely gone, Stephen smiled at the administrator. "Thankfully, I have well-trained staff; they will extract the experiments without any undue danger. After that, I will need to do exit interviews with each member of the staff."

"Of course." The administrator nodded nervously. "How should I instruct my staff?"

"Gather them on the top floors of the building, and we will come to retrieve you when the extraction is complete."

The administrator left, and Stephen turned to the others.

"All right. Arisha, you go with Ruslan, Stoyan with Aibek. Show them how this is done. The extraction point is where we came down."

The four of them nodded and disappeared.

Stephen?

Yes, my Queen?

How is your operation going?

Proceeding well. Stephen tried to come up with something to say that would sound less curt. *I will be glad when I have seen the last of these slimy, self-absorbed administrators. None of them have any remorse. We've found a few scientists who might be able to be recruited, but all in all, I fear this program is a scathing indictment of humanity.*

And this *is why I don't spend much time on Earth,* Bethany Anne told him promptly. *The people seem to go out of their way to make me question the idea of saving them from intergalactic war.*

Stephen laughed at that. *I can't argue with that. In any*

case, this stage is nearly done, and then we'll deal with our vigilante friend. He tried to double-cross us to get to the facilities first, so I'm beginning to doubt that this will have a pleasant resolution.

Yes, I hear Jennifer had to challenge an alpha at the latest facility—someone hell-bent on getting the revenge this Emeric person promised them.

What?

Yes, our little girl is all grown up and may or may not come back with a pack in tow.

I-I just...what?

"Jennifer would like to clarify that this is a temporary arrangement, and it was not so much an alpha challenge as a non-lethal fight to determine who would command the mission into the Naftalan facility," ADAM informed them both.

Uh-huh. Stephen no longer saw any of the landscape. *Well, I'm going to go back to what is apparently the boring sort of extraction, and I'll see you all later.*

He went to debrief the scientists with Bethany Anne's delighted laughter ringing in his mind.

Naftalan, Azerbaijan

"This is the last facility, you know," Irina said, as the small party wound their way down the road to the gates. "Perhaps we should say a few words to mark the occasion."

"Nope," Jennifer replied. "Get in, get out, blow it up... and maybe then I'll say a few words. But only when it's a smoking wreck."

Zurya smiled. Though she was still inclined not to look

favorably on Jennifer, she knew that their interests were aligned at least in this.

In truth, Zurya had been terrified about storming the facility—afraid that she would see her family slaughtered before her eyes, or that they would see her killed.

Emeric had assured them that if their family was saved by this other group—the group with the vampire—that they would be sent back to a life of drudgery, forever harmed, and they would all have to sit by while the perpetrators were free to do the same again. She could not bear that thought.

Now that she saw how her fear had been used against her, she found the courage to admit to herself that she no longer had any place as an alpha. With so many of their warriors gone, the pack had clung to her as the one constant. And Zurya had let them down.

She resolved that she would not seek to become alpha again when this woman left.

They reached the gates, and Hsu took center stage. She swiped her card and frowned when the gates did not open.

Then they noticed the wire—the gates had been bound closed. The land between the gates and the facility was covered with recently-disturbed piles of dirt. The facility was entirely closed off. The people inside had set up a defensive perimeter.

"ADAM," Jennifer demanded urgently. "Tell me what's going on in there."

"Unfortunately, this facility did not have video surveillance enabled. The repair record shows that they have had extensive electrical problems caused by rodents chewing on the wires. I have not been able to see inside the facility to see any arrangement of weapons or defensive capabilities. I can say from infrared, however, that there are live bodies in cages."

Jennifer relaxed slightly. At least the strange defensive positioning of this facility was not combined with killing the Wechselbalg outright.

Yet.

She knew she needed to approach this very carefully.

"Try talking to them," she told Hsu in an undertone.

Hsu nodded and pressed the intercom button.

There was a crackle from the radios. "Get away!" The voice was male, high with fear, and it strengthened into a furious hiss the next moment. "We're armed. You won't win. The facility is closed."

Jennifer snorted slightly at the thought that this man could win against them, but Hsu was, thankfully, unflappable.

"I am aware of the orders you received," Hsu said calmly. "This is Chief Administrator Zhang. I was sent here by Hugo to help make sure the staff could be evacuated safely."

"I don't believe you! I know the truth about Hugo."

"What's his name?" Hsu asked Jennifer quietly.

"Zhaparov," ADAM informed them. "At least, it was as of the latest official transmission."

Jennifer relayed this and Hsu nodded. She pitched her voice to be low and persuasive. "Is this Administrator Zhaparov?"

"Go *away!*"

The line cut.

"Huh," Jennifer said after a moment.

Nikhil Zhaparov huddled down in the corner of his office, eyes locked on the phone in the corner of the room.

He was ready for them, he told himself. His fingers were wrapped around the barrel of the gun, and he kept leveling it at the door and trying to aim it quickly. He was shaking, of course, but he'd be able to do it if they broke in.

Right?

On the table lay the transmission, the one he should never have been able to access. When Nikhil was assigned here, to lead a facility that was entirely cut off from the world, he had made sure to learn everything he could about how to get information into the facility...and restrict information going out.

He sabotaged the security cameras time and again, and sometimes other electronics, carving the little power cords up in a pattern to look like mice had chewed at them. He installed a small satellite dish on the grounds, inside a stack of supply crates. He never confided in anyone.

He was not stupid. He knew that someone who did secret research for an eccentric billionaire might end up wealthy beyond all imagining...or dead in a ditch with no fingerprints.

He had every intention of escaping the latter.

When he first received the message from Hugo, telling them that they should prepare to close and that all of them would be given recommendations, he knew enough to be wary.

Who in their right mind would release this many staff back into the world? Who would trust nine whole facilities' worth of staff not to blab about where they had been working or what they had been doing? As it was, every communication outside of the facility was monitored.

No, Hugo would never close this all down and let them go. They would end up in another of his facilities...or dead.

So, Nikhil investigated and found that Hugo Marcari was dead.

Again, he was not stupid. He considered many possibilities. Perhaps Hugo Marcari had been an assumed name, a stolen identity. Perhaps he had faked his death. Perhaps he just wanted to go underground for a while.

But perhaps he truly was dead, and someone else was sending messages as him. Either way, Nikhil did not like his chances if they got into the facility.

Eventually, they would need a source for supplies, and a way to get out of here safely—or, at least, he would. He'd always accepted that the others might end up dead at the end of this. If it came to it, he had no problems leaving them to die.

The question was, how to make the people at the gates leave?

He should have been calmer. He should have told them that he was happy to have them come in, and then he should have run while they were occupied with the others.

His eyes drifted to the handgun and the grenades nearby.

If they got in, he wasn't going to let them kill him. He'd do it himself first.

Not that he had to resort to that just yet...but it was good to know.

He watched through a window as the party at the gate

waited for a bit, then made their way back up the hill. He breathed a sigh of relief. He was safe for now.

Sofia, Bulgaria

"This is a terrible idea," Dedov hissed down into the darkness.

There was no response except for the sounds of breathing and scraping as Milen climbed carefully into the bombed-out husk of the building.

It groaned faintly with every footstep. They had even heard it groaning as they walked up the hill, but no amount of angry mutters from Dedov made Milen turn back. The man seemed blind to danger.

And Dedov...well, Dedov didn't want the man to think he was a coward. He also didn't know his way back to the city.

He was a coward, though. He was frozen at the edge of the building, having scraped his hands scrambling up the wall, and he wasn't brave enough to step out onto the loose stones that led down the building. He squeezed his eyes shut and prayed for the courage to move one way or the other—into the darkness of the building, or back to the city.

Arisha had been here, though.

That got him into motion. If tiny little Arisha, with her pert face and her curvy body, had been scrambling around in here, he could too. He wouldn't be outdone by her. She'd never respect him if he said he'd not been brave enough to even enter the facility.

He levered himself down carefully and edged down the slope.

"Are you coming?" a voice called from the darkness.

Dedov spared the darkness an annoyed glance. "*Yes.* Be patient."

One more step, and another. His foot slid slightly, and he froze, almost vomiting with fear. But the slope held, and he kept moving. He could do this. He *was* doing this. He steadied himself on a beam and kept moving into the shadows cast by the moonlight.

He could hear his own rough breathing, and a strange excitement pounded through him. He'd never done anything like this, and it was exhilarating.

Then it happened.

His foot caught, his ankle twisted, and he tumbled into the darkness. He hit the remnants of a wall face-first, and a pained yell burst out of him.

But he had too much momentum. Even as he scrambled for a handhold, he toppled sideways and down the slope.

He could sometimes see the sky as he rolled end over end, but a few seconds later, even that was gone. Milen was calling his name, and Dedov tried to call for help, but his throat was closed with fear. He could hear only his own muted whimpering noises as he grabbed for rocks, chunks of wood—anything to stop his slide. His coat tore on something.

Finally, he came to a stop.

Dedov picked his head up slowly and found himself sprawled on a flat surface. He gave a low moan of pain and fear.

In the absolute blackness, and with the groan of the

unstable building above him, he slumped back down— tears hot on his face.

"Dedov!" The voice was panicked and distant. "Use your flashlight! Climb back up!"

The flashlight. Of course. Dedov fumbled in his coat and could have cried when he realized it was still there. He pressed the button awkwardly and squinted against the sudden white beam of light.

He turned, trying to find the slope...

And stopped dead.

There, on a still-upright wall, were unmistakable bloodstains. And next to them, the stone had been raked by huge claws.

The wolves had been here.

Naftalan, Azerbaijan

"I'm setting the Pod down on top of the roof. Descend very carefully, so your footsteps are not heard."

"Thank you, ADAM," Stephen said. "And you'll send the Pod back for Jennifer and the rest?"

"Of course. I have no wish to see Jennifer attempt to navigate a minefield."

"You feel those emotions?" Stephen's brows lifted. "That's... You know, I can't tell whether or not that's comforting."

"A question for another time, perhaps."

Stephen stepped out into the afternoon air with a smile. He could not help but feel happy about the fact that this was the last facility.

Naryn had been wrapped up very quickly. Aibek and Ruslan withdrew to the *ArchAngel* with their families, Aibek cradling a small child in his arms with an expression that said he could see nothing else in the whole world.

Ruslan had taken temporary charge of the pack, though Stephen could tell that Ruslan had a very similar outlook to Nathan. He had a deep and almost overwhelming sense of responsibility for his pack and would happily do whatever needed to be done in a crisis, but he was also happy to be a second-in-command. Ruslan, Stephen thought, did not like the drama and hassle that would come with being the alpha of a pack—and as a second-in-command, he would never have to bargain with other pack leaders or deal with the minutiae of petty disputes between pack members.

Secure in the knowledge that he was leaving the Wechselbalg in good hands, Stephen had taken a moment to watch the families reunited, and the remaining Wechselbalg from Khachmaz already looked happier and more settled.

With that image in his head, he, Arisha, and Stoyan took a Pod and headed to Naftalan.

"We are on our way," he told Jennifer.

"Thank God." Her voice was emphatic in his earpiece. "This one's a shit show. The guy's gone crazy."

"Well, Hugo couldn't be the only crazy one." Stephen had grinned as he settled back in his seat in the Pod. He gave a glance to where Arisha and Stoyan were whispering together, as new lovers were wont to do, and gave a rueful shake of his head.

No matter how many centuries he lived in, people seemed to be all the same.

Now, with the wind above and the frozen, landmine-strewn earth below, Stephen watched as the Pod shot straight up out of sight and returned in an almost-invisible blur. If he were human, he was not sure he would have seen it.

Jennifer's party climbed into the Pod and climbed out cautiously a few moments later on the roof of the facility.

Everyone, Stephen was happy to see, followed ADAM's instructions to be quiet.

He nodded to the former alpha of Jennifer's new pack, a woman with grey-and-white hair and piercing black eyes. She nodded back, if not happily, then at least courteously.

"So, what's the situation?" he asked Jennifer quietly.

She took her time walking to join him, letting her feet land softly and deliberately.

"The administrator is holed up in his office," she explained. "It looks as if everyone else is sheltering in place. He wanted us to leave and refused to talk to us. He says he knows the 'truth' about Hugo. It was on the news, so I suppose we had to expect that someone would find out sooner or later."

Stephen nodded. "The facilities were supposed to be closed off, but a smart administrator would make sure they had a conduit to the outside world. The question is, what's his plan now?"

"I've been thinking about that." Jennifer shielded her gaze from the sun and looked at him, her blue eyes unexpectedly grave. "If you're him, you know people are coming and you think they're going to kill you, and you know you won't be getting any more supplies, how would you try to get everyone out safely? You're on a time limit, remember."

"I don't think you can get everyone out safely," Stephen

said bluntly. "Surely he must realize that this is his last stand."

"Not if he intends to go out with a bang," Jennifer replied grimly. "*Or* if he intends to let them be cannon fodder and leave on his own. Those are the only two feasible plans."

"Throw them under the bus and..." Stephen shook his head. "Yeah. I think you might be right. Unfortunately for him, I don't think we're going to leave him any space to slip away."

Jennifer grinned but sobered quickly. "Here's the deal. They've had a lot of electrical problems at this facility, but never ones affecting the labs or the experiments. Always things to do with surveillance and communications. ADAM thinks this guy was also taking down the automated systems Hugo used to spy on people."

Stephen's mind made the leap easily. "So, what else has he added in?"

"Exactly." Jennifer nodded. "What the hell else are we going to find in there? ADAM *was* able to get rid of the automated poison systems and all of that, but what if he's put in secondary systems we can't touch? We haven't had the time for him to do a complete technical readout of the building, and frankly, I'm not sure we can afford to wait."

Stephen nodded, "You're right. A strike team to the administrator's office, I think. Get the truth out of him—what I wouldn't give for Barnabas about now—and take the rest of the facility."

"Sounds good." Jennifer nodded decisively. She beckoned to the older woman. "This is Zurya. Zurya, Stephen. If you can come with us, we'll leave the rest of the people

TO HELL AND BACK

here, infiltrate to the administrator's office, and find out what's going on in there."

Zurya nodded. "I'm on board." She hesitated. "And as much as I hate to say it, you're doing better than I would be."

Khachmaz, Azerbaijan

The little plane touched down near Khachmaz in the early afternoon, and Emeric left the pilot with money for fuel. He was not certain if he would need a ride back, but he wanted a loyal pilot if he did.

The journey through the underbrush to the meeting place went quickly, and he was there long before the team he had radioed for rendezvous: local pack members, all of them searching for their loved ones.

He buttoned on a lab coat as he walked. It barely fit across his shoulders, but it made a good enough disguise. People were only too willing to write off scientists as a threat. In Emeric's experience, that was a big mistake.

The scientists at Gordes had been sadists, every one of them. Even the ones who were shocked when they first arrived quickly turned their coats to save their own skins.

That was why he was determined to see the humans pay. Over the years, he had heard many justifications about why the Unknown World must keep itself hidden. Always, he was told that humans would not understand. That there would be fear and violence. That it was simply easier to stay hidden and lay low than to try to reach for more.

And all that boiled down to was that humans were cruel at heart. Emeric had seen resentment fester even in the

NATALIE GREY & MICHAEL ANDERLE

non-shifter descendants of the pack lines. Humans could not stand for other beings to have powers they did not have, and because they could not stand it, they tried to control it the way they would control a horse or a dog.

Five minutes past the rendezvous time. He checked his watch.

Were they not coming? If not, why not?

His heart sinking, he crept forward and scanned through the greenery to see the facility.

Everything looked normal. There were no streaks of blood on the ground or bodies...

He kept moving, scanning the wall and looking back occasionally at the still-empty rendezvous point. Nothing seemed out of place, but his instinct told him that something was wrong.

Was it possible that TQB had been here already? No, they wouldn't have had time.

Right?

He reached the gates and saw nothing out of the ordinary. There were some frozen tracks through the mud, the treads of the supply trucks immortalized in the dirty field that surrounded the building.

On a whim, he scanned the card he had gotten from Gerard. The light on the gate blinked green, and the big doors slid back into the wall itself.

No one spoke through the intercom. No one questioned him. Certain that something was wrong, he walked to the side doors of the facility, and he pulled them open with a jerk, ready for men with guns.

There were none. Nor was there screaming. Emeric walked down the hallway in eerie silence, checking each room as he passed. No dead bodies, and no live ones, either.

His steps quickened as he became increasingly sure that the facility was empty.

The second floor held the first set of labs, and he looked inside them to see every cage standing open. No signs of a struggle, as he would expect if Hugo's people had gotten here before him. Not the faintest speck of fresh blood.

No, they had gone willingly.

And that meant...

Emeric's jaw tightened. That meant the vampire had double-crossed him. He had promised to work with Emeric, then he had decided to take matters into his own hands.

He was going to pay for that.

He reached into his pocket and pulled out a phone, retreating to the outdoors for a signal.

"Sidonie? We have a problem."

QBS *ArchAngel*

Aibek cradled Gulnara in his arms. The personnel had told him apologetically that they were out of beds in the main medical bay, but that he could take her to one of the crew cabins.

Aibek didn't care. He sat on the floor of the med bay himself, holding his young niece and savoring the weight of her in his arms. She was still alive. She was real, and she was here, and she was all right.

Having shown a proclivity for being a shifter, she had been separated from the adults. In halting words, she described them trying to tell her to give up her independence and shift on command, to obey orders while in wolf form.

What she was too young to explain was how deeply *wrong* those orders felt—and while she couldn't explain it, Aibek knew exactly what she meant. A pack member did not simply obey anyone who asked for obedience. They obeyed their alpha and their alpha's representatives. At a young age, when Gulnara's shifting capabilities were hardly even developed enough to follow such commands, she still understood why she shouldn't.

And, if he understood her story correctly, she had lied to her captors with the exact angelic smile she used while stealing cookies. She told them she was trying to shift. She pretended to be their friend and trust them. But she made sure not to obey their orders all the time, and make it look as if she wasn't entirely sure what she was doing.

She wound them around her little finger, just like she did everyone else in real life, and he had never been so proud.

So proud, and so full of grief—because her parents were gone. Her father, Jehan, had fought too early and too much to try to get back to his wife and child, and had been killed in front of the other prisoners. His wife, Aibek's sister, Hana, had died of grief not long after, perhaps believing that Gulnara was dead, too.

Aibek's arms tightened involuntarily, and his niece stirred in his arms, half-waking from her slumber.

He loosened his grip with a murmured apology.

How was he going to rebuild this? How?

For a fleeting moment, he entertained the notion of

seeking out Emeric Carre and his associate. He would be dreaming of revenge for some time, after all, and why should he not have it?

It was his second-in-command who provided the answer. Ruslan crouched nearby, examining a young woman's arm. She had been patched up with the same near-magical treatments as everyone else and was smiling up at Ruslan gratefully. As Aibek watched, his friend helped the woman to her feet, and they went to check on her son.

They needed this, Aibek realized. They did not need to plunge into revenge and anger once again, they needed to rebuild. Launching attacks on human towns would get more of his kind killed, and those at the facility had already paid for their crimes—Aibek had watched them be judged.

His phone rang, somewhat incongruously. He had assumed they were out of range of his little network, but the technology on this ship was clearly beyond all under-standing for him.

It was Emeric's second-in-command, Sidonie.

Aibek put the phone back in his pocket and gathered Gulnara close once more.

He had all he needed.

Sofia, Bulgaria

Dedov hobbled up the incline. Adrenaline was pumping through him, and he could hardly speak.

"Dedov? *Dedov?*"

"I'm here!" He could barely force the words out, he was

breathing so hard, but he wanted to shout his excitement. "I'm all right!"

He had followed the hallway as far as he could, seeing wolf bodies and human bodies on the floor. Embarrassingly, he'd thrown up once—but no one had to know about that.

There had been computers and burned pieces of paper. He didn't think there was anything to salvage, and he certainly wasn't going to haul a server out, not up that slope. If Milen wanted it, he could go back for it.

But the wolves were real, and they truly were massive. A few times, when the building groaned, Dedov had thought he was hearing the growl of a wolf and had almost sobbed with fear.

No wolves appeared, however, and eventually he climbed up and out into the night, grabbing Milen's hand to haul himself onto a wall. His legs shook with exhaustion, but he could not remember ever feeling so alive.

Milen waited, trying to be patient but getting more and more intrigued as the minutes went on.

Finally, Dedov couldn't hold it in any longer—even to make the other man wait. "I found it. There were wolves down there. Not the height of a man's shoulder, maybe, but bigger than wolves should be. And there were human bodies, too."

"Anything about this place and who owns it?"

"The computers were destroyed," Dedov explained with a shrug. "There was a fire. Maybe from the bombing?"

"Maybe." Milen shook his head as they both looked at the black void of darkness at the center of the ruins. "I don't understand it. There were always ghost stories about this place, people would say they heard screaming, and now maybe there were wolves here, and...it's just unbelievable. Maybe the wolves got in and killed everyone, and that's what your friend knew about."

"Maybe." Dedov shook his head. "But why the bombing? Who did that part?"

"Maybe we'll find the connection in Spain," Milen suggested. "Because it looks like she went there, too."

Both of them jumped as the gunshot-sharp crack of wood was followed by a low groan and tumble of rock.

"Let's get off this wall," Milen suggested, with feeling. "We can make a plan back in Sofia."

"*Da.*"

As Dedov climbed down the wall, heedless of the danger to himself, all he could think about was the wolves.

The wolves that existed.

How had Arisha ever found out about this?

Naftalan, Azerbaijan

"I've opened the door for you."

"Thank you, ADAM." Stephen turned the handle on the door quietly, listening for the sounds that would indicate guards on the other side. He heard nothing and pulled the door toward himself as slowly as he could, stopping as soon as he heard a creak.

He edged around it and into the darkness.

No doubt the administrator had wanted to make it difficult for anyone who was not a worker at this facility to find their way around, but he hadn't counted on the fact that this particular set of opponents could see very well in dim light.

Stephen gave a feral smile and rolled his shoulders, feeling the gun's harness readjust.

At the stairs, they found their first complication: a metal stairway, almost certain to clang lcudly if they walked down it.

"These bastards," Stephen muttered. "Couldn't they afford concrete like everyone else?"

"Had to cut corners somewhere," Jennifer replied mournfully. "And of course, it wouldn't be the cages." She pointed to a shadow in one corner. "There's the poor, sad surveillance camera. I wonder how many times he killed them himself?"

Stephen shook his head, "Crazy is as crazy does." He paused. "Though I have to admit that on the subject of mistrusting Hugo, this guy was spot on."

"You know, that's a good point," Jennifer agreed.

"Not to interrupt," Zurya said calmly. "But how are we going to get down?"

"Oh. I had an idea." Stephen headed for the railing. "If this doesn't work...well, get ready to fight."

He climbed carefully over the railing and worked his way down until he hung from the edge of the concrete landing. He took a moment to scope the next landing below swung his body a few times and dropped silently.

"It worked," he called up, as quietly as he could.

"You go next," he heard Jennifer say to Zurya.

The Wechselbalg landed next to him a few moments later. She stood up and brushed off the knees of her pants, then offered him a hand. They waited as Jennifer dropped, rolled, and cursed slightly when she slid into a wall.

"How are you pure death in a battle and so uncoordinated outside of one?" Stephen teased her.

"The same way *you're* a perfect gentleman most of the time and a total ass other times." She stuck out her tongue at him.

"I am—" Stephen began, but she cut him off with a grin.

"Let's argue it out in that restaurant in Paris."

"It's hard to stay mad at you when you have such good ideas."

Stephen listened at the door for a moment. He could hear faint movement in the building. Even when people were quiet, small actions reverberated through to form a small hum of background noise. But were there footsteps?

"ADAM, can you tell me if there are any guard patrols nearby?"

"Yes, one patrolling the outside corridor of this floor," ADAM reported. "Or at least, two humans circle regularly. You are presently at the southwest corner facing north, while they are at the northeast and circling clockwise. You could most likely reach the administrator's office, which is along the north side, without the guards spotting you."

"Huh." Stephen peered out the window. To his left, the corridor turned north. "Head to the left and be quiet," he told them, for Zurya's benefit. "Guards are patrolling."

He eased the door open, and the team slipped out.

"We should wait here," he told the others as softly as he could and still be audible. "I'd rather not have them circle around and complicate matters while we're trying to question the administrator."

"Yes, that would be...bad," Jennifer agreed.

Zurya simply nodded.

It wasn't long before even a human could have picked up the tramp of boots. The guards were walking in lockstep, talking quietly about... Stephen strained to hear. What were they discussing?

Their favorite actresses.

Stephen, who had been the paramour of quite a few

prima donnas in his day—not to mention quite a few ambitious understudies—could only shake his head. The women of the stage in past years had been intelligent, well-educated, daring. One *had* to be daring, after all, to risk the censure of society at large. Every one of them had been free spirits, as cunning in pursuit of fame as any banker in pursuit of money.

It just wasn't the same anymore. Actresses today were little more than pretty, in his opinion. He had yet to see a single tabloid photo that brought to mind the larger-than-life personalities he had encountered in his younger years.

Of course, they had also been prone to trying to kill him in his sleep after finding out about his dalliances with the understudies...

As the footsteps drew closer, Stephen allowed his claws to extend. Jennifer and Zurya stepped back, and the moment the guards turned the corner, Stephen was in motion.

The guards' lives ended in gurgles as his claws took them in the throat.

He didn't bother to move the bodies. With stairways at each corner, they were likely to be seen no matter where he left them, and they were against the clock now. He jerked his head to Jennifer and Zurya, and the three of them slipped down the corridor toward the administrator's office.

In the dark of the office, Nikhil's eyes were locked on the door. The panic button was nearby, easy to press and release the poison if he needed to do so, and his gun was solid and comforting in his hands.

In twenty seconds, the patrol should come around again.

In the past few days, he had learned the mannerisms of each patrol. The first shift walked slowly, dawdling in a way that made Nikhil want to kill them. The second shift tended to vary their speed, sometimes moving fast and other times strolling along, though their salutes were always crisp when they saw him. He figured there was no harm in irregularity. But he liked the third shift best. Their circuit varied by no more than one or two seconds. They were creatures of precision, just like him.

Ten seconds until the patrol came around again.

When he got out, he didn't even know which direction he would go. If he set out into the wilderness, he might confound anyone looking for him. On the other hand, the reason they would expect him to go into town was that it was the only sensible thing to do in the middle of winter. He didn't have cold weather gear, a map, or supplies.

The patrol should appear in...

He frowned, took a deep breath. Counted to three. Counted to three again.

They had never been this late.

Had there been a shift change? He shifted his gun in his hands anxiously and felt himself begin to shake. Where was the patrol? He hadn't heard the stairwell door open and close, or footsteps on the metal. None of the building's alarms blared.

Maybe they were testing him, teasing him. Maybe they

thought it was funny how he was holed up in here. Nikhil grimaced.

But fear was a strong motivator. Carefully, so carefully that he hardly made a sound, Nikhil crawled toward the door.

He couldn't hear anything outside. No footsteps. Half his brain insisted that the patrol was dead, and the other half told him not to be ridiculous. The group hadn't come back to the gates, and he'd placed people at every window to watch the walls.

There was no way anyone was getting in here without him knowing about it.

He silently rose to look out the little window and saw nothing. Then he opened the door as quietly as he could and peeked into the hallway. Still, he saw nothing, so he took a few steps out, trying to listen over the sound of his heart.

He decided to go to the right first. He peered into the stairwell and saw nothing—nothing, nothing, always nothing—and then looked down the hall.

He froze.

The guards *were* dead. They had been killed so quietly that he hadn't heard them, and there were puddles of blood spreading out beneath their bodies.

A scream built in his throat as he scrambled for the door of his office. He had to get the door locked, he had to be safe, he had to get to the panic button—

He was slammed sideways as he entered the room. The gun went skittering away across the floor, and he flipped, landing on the floor on his shoulder. Hands forced him down and then wrenched his head up.

A brown-haired man sat behind Nikhil's desk. His clothing was neat and fashionable, his features handsome and clear-cut, his smile genuinely amused as he watched Nikhil laid out on the floor. He tilted his head to the side as Nikhil panted in abject terror.

"Hello," said the man. "Administrator Zhaparov, I presume?"

Jennifer held the administrator down on the floor, his arm twisted behind his back. For someone holed up in an office with a dozen loaded guns, he'd been surprisingly easy to take down.

This was the guy who wanted to leave the rest of the facility to die while he escaped? It seemed that intention and ability were very separate things in this case. The man was practically reduced to jelly, shaking on the floor as he tried to crane his head to see Jennifer.

She kept her fingers clenched in his hair, and his face turned firmly toward Stephen.

"Do you know why I am here?" Stephen asked the man. He had stopped looking at the administrator and was examining the panic button—now severed from any connecting wires. He looked back at the man.

"N-no," the man stammered, beginning to cry.

"I am here," Stephen explained plainly, "because you have engaged in the systematic torture of dozens of people."

There was a long pause.

"You're not even going to attempt to deny it?" That would be somewhat refreshing.

"I knew you weren't from Hugo," the man whispered. "I knew this was all a trap. What did you do to him?"

Stephen nodded over his head at Jennifer.

"I tore him limb from limb," Jennifer replied. She tilted her head to look at the man. "You see, I can shift into a wolf, too."

The man gave an involuntary scream.

"Now, now. There's no need for that." Stephen drummed his fingers on the desk. "So, let us talk about what you did under Hugo's orders, hmm? You attempted to force Wechselbalg to shift into their wolf forms and take orders—both of which would be considered gravely immoral. Why did you feel justified in doing so?"

"They aren't human," the man gasped out. He remembered too late that Jennifer was the one holding him down and gave a gulp of terror. "They aren't the same as—oh, god, you're one of them, too, aren't you?"

Stephen let his eyes deepen to red, the claws extend from his fingertips, and his fangs grow. Just for a moment, and then he faded back to his normal self.

"No," he replied simply.

The man was sobbing now.

"What, no justification? No courage? No acknowledgment?" Stephen stood up and strolled from behind the desk. "You're the last one, did you know that? Every one of your fellow administrators is dead. A few scientists and guards dared to defy their orders and put their lives on the line to help the shifters, but I'm certain you didn't.

"So, are you going to tell me again that it was all justified because someone in power gave you the right to hack people open and give them commands that you enforce with torture? Or are you going to tell me what Hugo did: that most of the world is simply meant to take orders? Or something else, perhaps?

"Why did you do it?"

The man let his head rest against the floor for a moment before he craned his neck to look at Stephen again.

"No progress has ever been made without suffering," he replied. "How do you think we've found cancer treatments and weapons and all of that? It's just how it is. You can stand aside and not do it, but it will still get done. I didn't care about any of Hugo's ideas about nobles and commoners, but why shouldn't I be the one making money if he was only going to get someone else when I said no?"

There was not even a moment of realization in his eyes as Jennifer cut his throat in one quick movement.

She let his body drop to the floor and stood, her face impassive as she stared down at him.

"He wasn't going to say anything useful," she told Stephen flatly. Her body shook. "Someone else will torture people, so why shouldn't I get paid to do it? This whole thing makes me sick," she whispered.

Stephen wrapped her in his arms.

He had never meant to upset her by drawing this out. Thoughtless cruelty seemed a more malevolent force than all the willful evil in the world.

"Come on." He sighed. "Let's finish this and go home."

Jennifer leaned against him, taking comfort in the feel

of her face pressed up against his chest and the strength of his arms around her.

"I didn't ask him to speak because—" Stephen began, but she cut him off with a smile and a finger over his lips.

"I know why you asked," she told him. "Deep down, some part of you still wants the world to be a good place. And maybe sometimes it is. But sometimes we have to fight to make it that way." She laced her fingers through his. "Come on. You were right. Let's finish it and go home."

17

Naftalan, Azerbaijan

"Are you sure about this?" Stephen asked Jennifer in an undertone.

The last Pod was loading. Stoyan helped Arisha and Hsu into it. The rest of the Wechselbalg, including Zurya, had already left for the *ArchAngel*, along with a shell-shocked young scientist who the Wechselbalg had pointed out as a kind member of the team.

The woman had apparently been locked in a cage herself, ready to be used as the bait in one of the experiments—this was after she had tried to stage an escape.

That sort of courage was inspiring when you remembered that she was aware that had she allowed other people to suffer, she could survive.

Perhaps she would sign on with TQB.

Stephen looked at Jennifer now, nodding to the Pod when she frowned. "You could go back up there, take a nice bath, I'll handle everything at Naftalan and—"

"I'm fine, really." Jennifer smiled up at him. "I'm sorry I got all flustered."

"Nothing to apologize for when you're dealing with sociopathic mass murderers," Stephen pointed out. "It's a distressing subject."

Jennifer gave a chuckle and waved to the inhabitants of the Pod as the door slid closed.

"So," Irina spoke from behind them. She was bouncing on the balls of her feet, impatient to get going. "Let's go talk some sense into this man."

"You're very hopeful," Jennifer observed. "You really think he'll be reasonable? He's probably found out about Khachmaz at this point."

"He wants revenge," Irina said, lifting her shoulder. "But this isn't the heat of the moment, is it? It's not like when the red comes down over your eyes, and you can't think of anything except tearing a person to shreds. He's had days to calm down."

Stephen was skeptical.

Still, he wanted Irina here. Jennifer had only faced the forced transformation once, and by accident. Irina was the one who could fully empathize with Emeric. She might be able to change his mind in a way no one else could.

"Let's go, then." A Pod descended, and they climbed in.

Behind them, the bodies were being taken away, but Stephen did not even turn to watch.

Finally, it was over.

Sofia, Bulgaria

It was perhaps two hours later that Dedov hunched over a mug of some mulled drink, letting his hands thaw.

He was still on a high from going into the bombed-out building, and not even his aching feet or bruised limbs could take that away. The walk back in the snow, despite the growing dark and cold, had been filled with moments when he wanted to laugh aloud.

Was *this* why Arisha did what she did? This high? Dedov could never imagine sitting in an office all day again. He'd go mad.

Milen returned from the bar with a plate of dumplings, a basket of brown bread, and a mug of tea for himself.

He looked more serious than Dedov did, almost pensive.

He sat down and chewed on a bite of brown bread thoughtfully.

"There were rumors," he said finally. "About Stoyan. Rumors that he wasn't quite normal. That he..." The man broke off and continued chewing.

"Which one was Stoyan?" Dedov was having trouble tracking the names through the man's thick accent. Bulgarians, it seemed, could not be relied upon to speak good Russian anymore.

"Stoyan was the muscle Filip brought in," Milen explained. "It was for a meeting with an American who was staying at the Hotel Sofia."

"Arisha talked about that hotel," Dedov interjected eagerly.

"Oh? Did she talk about the King Suite?" Milen asked sarcastically.

"Actually…yes." Dedov nodded. "She did. I assumed—well, how expensive is that suite?"

"More than a reporter can afford," Milen replied. "And the American was staying there, so if she said she saw it, then she saw him. And he saw Filip—I think, anyway, because Filip disappeared after going to that meeting."

"With Stoyan," Dedov clarified. "Who you think is…crazy?"

"Oh, no, not crazy." Milen shook his head. "There are many old rumors around here, rumors of people who can turn into beasts. Like the stories about the big wolves in the forest your grandmother used to tell you when you wouldn't eat your potatoes."

Dedov snorted amusement. He took a dumpling and chewed, wishing he had a nice vodka to wash it down, but enjoying the warmth from the mulled wine too much to let the cup go.

"Let me guess," Milen shot back. "You told your grandma you were too old for those stories, and she told you that you were a stupid little boy who didn't know anything about the world."

"Yes, actually." Dedov took a sip of his wine. "I guess grandmas aren't so different here, huh?"

"No." But Milen looked serious. "And I'm beginning to think maybe they're right about those things."

"*What?*" Dedov forced a laugh. The man was going mad, clearly.

"Listen." Milen leaned in. "You told me you saw, with your own eyes, wolves that were too big to be natural. You said you saw them. You saw the claw marks and how they'd killed people. So, if the wolves are real, why not the rest of it?"

"Maybe the wolves were made in a lab," Dedov said awkwardly. He didn't like this. The back of his neck was prickling. "Like those chickens that are so big."

"Then why have there been stories about them for centuries?" Milen demanded. "I told myself I was crazy, but then *you* saw them, and you don't believe in them, either! So, you give me a better explanation that accounts for all of this. Because right now it looks like Stoyan's one of those shifters—the ones who become giant wolves."

"That's crazy," Dedov stated flatly. He held up a hand to stave off his companion's protest. "Look, I'll give you the fact that the wolf was too big. Arisha was even looking into that. Maybe they're natural, maybe they're not. But the idea that just because I saw a big wolf, we *have* to believe they're also shifters? It's too much."

"Then ask your friend," Milen suggested. He jerked his head at Dedov's phone. "Just do this one thing. Tell her you've been looking into her research, and you think you've found the same thing. Tell her about the facility. And don't say you found wolves, say you found *shifters*. See what she says."

"What if she thinks I'm crazy?"

"Say you misspoke." Milen lifted a shoulder carelessly. "Get home and say you'd been drinking too much vodka with your babushka. I don't care. Just *ask*."

Dedov thought back to the old stories, to the way the world had seemed wild and dangerous when he was younger. It was the way he'd felt today, climbing into the darkness of the building, seeing the body of a beast that couldn't exist.

It felt right, somehow. More real than real life.

"Fine." He picked up his cell phone and dialed Arisha's number.

"*Da?*" She picked up after two rings.

"Arisha." Dedov smiled. "It's Dedov."

Naftalan, Azerbaijan

The sun had gone down by the time they arrived at Naftalan. They were able to land on the main grounds of the facility this time, so they didn't have to duck through the trees to try to approach invisibly.

"It's a bit nice being back here," Stephen said quietly. He shrugged. "I like it better when it's quiet, anyway."

"Were there any here who were…who did good things?" Irina looked around. The bodies had been taken away, a fact that chilled her somewhat even if she understood the necessity. She found herself hoping that someone here had been like Hsu.

"Four guards," Stephen said. He sounded impressed. "They volunteered for night shifts, and every night they would come and check on people, give them medical treatment, check on the children for the parents. They couldn't save many, but they were stockpiling supplies in the basement to try to make a run for it with the shifters."

Irina smiled. "That's good."

She would thank them when she returned to the *Arch-Angel*. She always thanked the ones who had helped, although the woman from Naryn had been so terrified that

Irina didn't want to give her a heart attack by shaking her hand.

The facility was eerily quiet, however. Their footsteps echoed on dirty floors, the wind whistled strangely through the halls—no one had thought to close the doors when they left—and the blinking computer screens, the last remnant of systems downloaded, wiped, and scrubbed by ADAM, made the light flicker.

"Do you think he's actually coming?" Jennifer asked as they climbed the stairs. She considered. "Or maybe he's going to ambush us."

"He's welcome to try," Stephen replied with a grin. "That would eliminate all doubt about how nice I should be to him."

"He's not there?" Bethany Anne asked.

"No," Stephen subvocalized. "At least as far as we can tell. There's no vehicle nearby, and none approaching."

"It's not possible that someone could have gotten in and out without ADAM noticing, is it?" Bethany Anne asked. She hesitated. "Unless—"

"Unless one of the others from the local group stayed," Stephen said quietly. "I'd have noticed Emeric if he was here, but what if he's just sending an emissary?"

"That Sidonie woman, maybe?"

"I'd have recognized her, too." Stephen frowned.

There was nothing as they made their way through the corridors. They checked each room, listening for sound despite ADAM's assurances that their bodies were the only warmth in the building.

Then they reached the administrator's office.

The note lay folded on the desk, a single slip of white

paper that had not been there when Stephen left the facility.

It was never your place to come here, the note read. *You betrayed the bargain. You betrayed those who should have been able to have their own revenge. But you have already lost. Your methods have made the people of the Unknown World your enemies. They know now what you have denied them. They know now that you cannot protect them.*

They will not be denied. Watch the storm you have created, for you are powerless to stop it. —E

Stephen folded the note and looked at Irina, who only shook her head.

"Why does he think humans have courts and lawyers and jails? The government cannot always protect you. Sometimes the most it can do is punish those who did the wrong thing."

"I think he's far beyond that kind of logic now," Jennifer replied. She shrugged. "On the plus side, we got all of them. He didn't manage to get to one of these facilities before we did, and we were able to talk those he did get to into joining our side."

"That's it!" Stephen looked around at her.

"What? What's 'it'?"

"I couldn't figure out what he meant to do. He clearly means to do something, doesn't he?" Stephen held up the note. "He says 'they will not be denied.' He says there's a storm coming.

"But those people are his weakness," Stephen stated quietly. He jabbed a finger for emphasis. "Those people are the ones who can tell us what he wants. He can't stand the thought of people like Irina, who was at those facilities, not wanting to rampage and kill every human they see. If the others complain that we wouldn't let them do what they wanted, he'll take them back...and we'll know what his plans are."

As if on cue, their earpieces crackled.

"Stephen, Jennifer, Irina—Stoyan would like to speak to all of you. He says one of the evacuees from Naryn has been contacted by Emeric," ADAM told them.

"Right on cue," Stephen murmured. He smiled at the other two. "Let's go figure out this guy's plans."

18

QBS *ArchAngel*

Stephen looked up as Aibek came into *ArchAngel*'s conference room. His niece, Gulnara, was still asleep in his arms and he gave an apologetic smile.

"I didn't want to wake her."

Stephen smiled and nodded as Aibek settled himself carefully into one of the conference room chairs.

"I hear you were contacted by Emeric," he began.

"Yes." Aibek grimaced. "I...lied to him."

Aibek was scared. It was clear from the way Stephen and the others behaved themselves that honor was considered important to them. He knew that his original acceptance of Emeric's offer had not been to their liking.

Still, he reassured himself, they had understood that. They had given him a chance to join their side.

Now, Stephen asked only, "What was the lie?"

"He asked how the extraction had gone." Aibek shot a worried look at his niece, afraid the story of her rescue would frighten her, but she slumbered on. "I told him that you had shown up and that we did not want to anger you, as you had more people and more weapons than we did. I told him that you had fixed our people up, though."

Stephen considered this. It was a self-serving lie in some ways, instead of the desperate truth Aibek had given him at the facility: that he would make a deal with anyone and anybody who would help him get his family back. On the other hand...

"Why did you lie?" Stephen tilted his head to the side and watched Aibek.

"I was scared." Aibek looked down at the table. "And... well, I failed, but I was trying to find out what he wanted to do next. He told me that we would need to help him with other attacks once we were done at the facility. I knew it was wrong, but I also knew I would be indebted to him. And I was angry. So I said we were angry at you, too. That you had my pack but that if we could sneak away, we would try to get revenge. All he would tell me was that the first attack was coming soon and that if we were back to talk to him in person after it, he might accept our help again. He...threatened me."

Aibek's fury was apparent to everyone in the room, but a moment later his shoulders sagged.

"We might be able to figure it out, however," Stephen said carefully. "What did he tell you about the attack? Exactly?"

"He told me that it would make a statement and show people that looking the other way wasn't the same as being blameless. He said he would hit the guilty people and scare them."

"The guilty people..." Stephen stared off into space. "Not the people at the facilities and not Hugo, as they're all dead. So who else is there? He talked about looking away. Maybe the people near the facilities?"

"Hugo also bribed numerous politicians," Jennifer said quietly.

"Good point." Stephen sank his chin onto one fist as he considered. "And he wants to scare people and make a statement. Would it make more of a statement to slaughter a village or kill a politician?" He shook his head. "There's a question I never thought I'd ask."

"I believe I might have found it," ADAM announced. "When Jennifer mentioned politicians, I began searching for politicians who might have been bribed by Hugo. One who has received many anonymous transfers of cash is giving an interview tomorrow in Madrid."

"I always forget how fast you work," Stephen said, amused. "And what do you think, ADAM, that he'd kill this man during the interview? Could he get there by tomorrow morning?"

"The interview is at noon, and I believe he is already en route back in the same plane."

"I don't suppose we could just take out the plane?" Jennifer asked.

"Unfortunately, there appears to be a pilot."

"Damn." She leaned forward on the desk and clasped her hands. "Is there any way to find out where Sidonie and the rest are?"

"I am not certain," ADAM responded. "After the trucks left Gordes, those in them dispersed. Some went into shopping centers or apartment buildings, and not all of *those* have video surveillance I can reach. Sidonie could have returned from Istaravshan by now, but it is difficult to know."

Jennifer squeezed her eyes shut.

"We can almost certainly track the phone that was used to call Aibek," ADAM offered. "The only way I would not be able to do that is if he were to turn it off. If he uses it to call anyone, I will inform you."

"Thank you, ADAM." Stephen laid his hands flat on the table and considered. "Everyone should be ready to leave within five minutes. I don't want to compromise our advantage by putting us in the middle of a busy city if that's *not* where the attack will be. It's just guesswork at this point."

Everyone nodded.

"Now, Arisha." Stephen looked at her. "You said you were going to Sofia?"

"Yes." Arisha raised her chin and ignored Stoyan's sudden look. "*Alone*," she added. She pushed herself up from the table and smiled at everyone, avoiding Stoyan's eyes. "I'll go get ready."

"And I," Stephen said quietly, "will go contact Jean-Marc Carre on the off-chance that he's heard from his son."

"I am also monitoring the roads into and out of Gordes," ADAM informed them. "I will let you know if there are any immediate changes."

"Excellent, thank you, ADAM." Stephen looked at the rest of them and felt a rush of pride. Every one of the people at this table was exhausted, with shadowed eyes and healing injuries. Every one of them had forced themselves to go into hell itself to free others, working through the night and the day without complaint, and they were nearly dead on their feet.

But they would keep fighting if he told them it was necessary. Not one of them would say a word about that. They would gear up and go to the next fight now if he asked them.

He was lucky to fight alongside such people.

"Get what little rest you can as soon as your gear is prepped," he told them. "All of you. Go on."

Arisha combed her hair with her fingers, trying to get the brown waves to settle into something approaching a reasonable hairstyle. A day and a half of racing through facilities while jumped up on adrenaline had made her look both tired and disheveled.

And she had to look attractive.

She knew from experience that looking desirable was one of the best ways to start a confrontation. With Dedov, who she'd caught looking at her more than once, looking good might confer a serious advantage.

She really needed that advantage, too. Dedov's call, and his accusations had terrified her to her core.

"You look...nice." Stoyan leaned in the doorway, his arms crossed. He frowned as he looked at her.

His face was so dark that she had to ask, "What?"

"Is this man an ex-boyfriend?" He raised an eyebrow.

Arisha burst out laughing. "Oh, God, no. I just know the best way to throw him off is to look nice. Of course, right now I think the best I can manage is not to look

NATALIE GREY & MICHAEL ANDERLE

like a huge mess. Everything I have to wear is covered in dirt."

Stoyan came in, wrapped her in his arms and kissed her. "You look beautiful," he told her. "Say you were hiking."

"In Bulgaria, in the middle of winter?" Arisha gave him a look. "No one goes hiking in the middle of winter."

"Ecaterina does," Jennifer called from the other room, where the others pored over communications that might shed light on Emeric Carre's plans.

"Uh...I don't know who that is, but...thanks?" Arisha looked at Stoyan and shook her head. "I just have to lie," she said simply. "That's all, I just have to lie."

"I want to go with you," Stoyan told her. "I want to protect you."

"We've been over this. You being there would be terrible. They know about you."

"Arisha, if you hadn't had that experience with the big wolf when you were little, what would you think when someone said werewolves were real?" Stoyan smiled. "You'd think they were crazy. If you ever said it, based on as little evidence as those people have, you'd also feel pretty embarrassed. They don't have to know any part of it is real. Having us both just laugh in their faces will show them that we're not frightened." He paused. "But, wait, what are you planning to tell him you were researching?"

Arisha gave him a small, secretive smile. "I'm telling him that I was conning the newspaper."

"I...don't get why that helps. It makes you look terrible."

"No, no, hear me out." Arisha held up a hand. "One thing he said was that he knew I had seen inside the big suites in the Sofia Hotel. I did write about them, so there's reason to think I was actually there. So, I'll say I padded my receipts for flights and so on so I could live it up on all of my trips. I'll offer him my post as a travel writer if he keeps his mouth shut."

"Uh-huh..."

"And he—because he's stupid—is going to try doing the thing I said I did and get caught. But by then I'll be long gone, and he'll have forgotten the werewolf thing." Arisha gave him a dimpled smile and returned to fixing her hair, giving herself a Cheshire cat smile in the mirror.

Stephen stuck his head around the door. "While I do approve of your plan," he said carefully. "You must remember that if this person doesn't believe your werewolf explanation, there will be problems. Promise me that if you can't get him to agree, you will get him somewhere safe so that we can wipe his memory."

"You wipe people's memories?" Arisha felt her heart flip over. "Like...mine? Are you going to wipe me?"

"No, absolutely not." Stephen shook his head. "You're part of the team. TQB has many humans on-staff. The issue is confidentiality. You want to help us. Dedov wants to expose us."

Arisha nodded.

"I'd like to go with her," Stoyan said.

"I told you—" Arisha began, but he shook his head.

"Hear me out. These are two men who are sure you're hiding something, and you said yourself that they're absolute jerks. I know you got away from Gerard, but I don't want to rely on any luck. They could slip something in your drink or hire some woman to lure you away or *any*thing. If they're sure you have some big secret and they want a payout, they're not going to behave well."

Arisha bit her lip and nodded.

"Just come back soon," Stephen told them both. "We may need everyone we can get to head off Emeric's plans."

Both nodded and left for the Pod bay.

With every step, Arisha replayed her conversation with Dedov.

"Dedov." She had felt a surge of adrenaline, mingled with a strange relief. Finally, this would come to a head. "Why are you calling?"

She did not mention that her cousin had told her of Dedov's visit.

"I am so glad to hear you are well." Dedov's tone was unctuous. "We all feared for you."

"Surely not." Arisha tried to laugh it off. "I haven't been gone very long. Viktor knew when I would be back."

"Viktor says he hadn't heard from you in days," Dedov said, although his confidence had clearly been shaken by her rebuttal. "He sent me to look for you."

"He must have missed the email. Anyway, I'm fine." Arisha forced a smile, even knowing that he couldn't see her. She had to project confidence.

"Arisha...I'm in Sofia." Dedov's voice was soft.

Her blood ran cold. "Why?"

"Tracking you."

"Surely Viktor told you that I was in Spain."

"He did." Dedov's voice took on a sly tone she didn't like. "But I admit, I volunteered for this and went to Sofia for a slightly different purpose. You see, Arisha, I know about the shifters."

She had to buy time to think up something good. "I think you cut out there. What did you say?"

"I know about the shifters," Dedov said impatiently.

"What shifters?" It was hardly a Grade A deflection, but it would do. "What are you talking about? Shifting what?"

There was a long pause.

"The wolves," Dedov said finally. "I know you've been researching wolves, and I know there were wolves near Sofia. Like from the old stories."

He knew far, far too much, but she wasn't about to give up. "Of course there are wolves," Arisha said. "They're all over. I think there's some kind of government cover-up." She cast about wildly for any sort of excuse. "I've been wondering if it's something to do with Chernobyl. They've been spotted all over. Anyway, I wasn't able to talk to many locals while I was in Sofia, but if you hear anything, let me know."

There was a silence, and she could only hope she had persuaded him.

"Come see me," Dedov had said. "Meet me in Sofia. We have a lot to talk about."

"Dedov, I have to get back to Moscow. Especially if they think I'm missing."

"Come to Sofia." His voice was soft and persuasive. "I'll make it worth your while. We can talk about what I've found out about the shifters."

And that decided it. Because she had to persuade him he was wrong.

"Fine. I'll change my flight. I'll tell you when I'm there."

Three hours later, she was ready. She had the plan. She had Stoyan with her.

She just had to persuade him.

193

Madrid, Spain

Julio Fraga whistled as he walked lightly down the stairs from his mistress's apartment.

It had been a good evening. He had presented her with a diamond necklace, and she had been even more gracious and charming than she normally was. She always greeted him at the door in a beautiful dress, with an elegant dinner laid out and the house perfectly arranged.

His wife wasn't a fan of the way Julio had taken to seeing Marisa since the payments started coming in. But they were rising in the world, and she had to understand that this was simply the way things would be now. After all, she hadn't complained when he bought *her* diamond necklaces, and she was able to start taking private tennis lessons and visiting the clubs.

He got to have his fun, too. Of course, he had indulged. Who wouldn't?

Then the real benefit of his office had begun. Payments arrived from all over, delivered over steak dinners from millionaires who murmured quietly that they would be *so* grateful if Julio would stop a regulation here, or look the other way there.

Of course, he had taken the bribes. Who wouldn't?

Now he was living the life he had always dreamed, and not even a jealous wife could dim his mood.

Tomorrow, he would begin campaigning for re-election. He would triumphantly announce it during his interview, and he could not wait to see his poll numbers surge.

Julio smiled as he hailed his driver and slid into the back seat of the limousine. Everything was going exactly as it should.

19

Sofia, Bulgaria

It was a little after ten in the evening when Arisha pushed her way into the lobby of the hotel Sofia.

She saw Dedov at once, and it only took a moment to see the second player in the act. Another man, short and blonde, sat at a table close by. Her heart skittered uncomfortably. What was he there for? To listen? To stop her from leaving?

She was glad that Stoyan was at her side, no matter how worried she was for his safety.

They made their way to Dedov's table and sat. Arisha was pleased to see a flicker of apprehension in his eyes at Stoyan's height and build.

Good.

"So what's going on?" Arisha hoped her look was one of pleasant confusion. "What were you saying on the phone?"

Dedov stared at her for a long moment. "Shifters," he

said finally as if he thought this might be a trap. "Werewolves."

Arisha stared at him with a look of—she hoped—confusion. She had to pretend that this didn't make sense to her at all. She opened her mouth, closed it again, and looked at Stoyan before biting her lip and looking back at Dedov. She hunched her shoulders, as if uncertain, and gave a small smile.

"Are you…this is a joke, right?"

"There have been rumors around here recently," Dedov insisted. "And I know you were looking at wolves."

"I told you, I've been looking into a government cover-up." Arisha leaned forward to whisper as if she were worried about being overheard. "If it is, this is dangerous, Dedov. There's a reason I didn't tell anyone about it. I thought…I thought I saw a wolf like that when I was little, that's all. So when I see those stories, I think they might be true. But it's not worth anyone getting *hurt* over."

"And that's what you've been hiding? With your trips?" Dedov looked around himself at the elegant lobby. "That can't be all. This place is far nicer than you said it was."

"Oh, come on." Arisha lifted a shoulder. "Spain, they're fine with me saying is all right. But they don't want anyone to say the post-Soviet countries are doing well. You should realize that."

"So there's…" Dedov frowned. "There's nothing?"

This was going to be easier than she had thought. Arisha smiled and leaned in close. "Look, I'll let you in on a secret, okay?"

Dedov leaned forward eagerly.

"I'm going to be leaving the newspaper," Arisha said.

She reached out and put her hand over Stoyan's looking at him with a smile. "I really liked the job. I got paid to travel around and stay in hotels. I got paid to go out to nightclubs and see how the drinks were! You have to write that it's all terrible, but it really isn't. I got vacations every couple of months. So when my job opens up, you should definitely apply for it."

Dedov stared at her, confused.

"In fact, I could tell Viktor I think you'd be good for it..." Arisha said persuasively.

Just then the man at the other table barged in on the conversation. He pointed at Stoyan, hand shaking.

"You're Stoyan," he said, through gritted teeth. "What happened to Filip? Tell me!"

Stoyan tensed, but to his credit, he responded admirably. Arisha watched as he frowned.

"Has something happened to Filip?" he asked carefully.

"He's missing," the man said. "And *you* know about it. And *you're* one of those shifters, aren't you?"

"Again with the—" Arisha looked between the two men and held her hands out. "I'm sorry if my research caused any confusion. I never meant you to be frightened by the old ghost stories." She shook her head at Dedov. "My grandmother gave me *nightmares*," she confided.

It was even true. Her grandmother's stories had been terrifying.

"I'm afraid I don't know about it," Stoyan said. He shook his head. "I was in Spain, with Arisha."

"Another benefit of traveling for work," Arisha murmured to Dedov in Russian, as if making an aside that neither of the other two at the table could understand.

"Companionship." She gave him a suggestive smile and looked back at Stoyan.

Stoyan was clearly trying not to laugh—even through his anger at the memory of Filip's betrayal. He lifted his shoulders in a helpless shrug.

"I didn't realize that Filip was missing," he said again. "I saw him a couple of weeks ago, and he seemed fine. Said he had a job, but he didn't need me for it."

"What about the American?"

"That was a bust." Stoyan shook his head. "Just a guy pretending to be an American businessman to get women."

"Oh." The other man sat down heavily. He seemed confused. "I was…I guess I was wrong."

"Filip will turn up," Stoyan said. "He always does, you know. Or maybe he's found a new gig out in the east somewhere. He did mention Tajikistan…"

Arisha stood, smiling brightly at Dedov. "I'm sorry I confused you so much," she said sweetly. "I'll let Viktor know I'm safe and I'm resigning. And you should definitely get that job." She showed him her dimples. "Enjoy your drink."

She and Stoyan walked back through the streets in silence, trying to hold in their laughter, but as soon as they were in the Pod, they broke down. Arisha held her hand up for a high five.

"Did you see their *faces*?"

Stoyan wiped at his eyes, chest shaking. "They're going to be searching Tajikistan for *months*. Do you know how many black-market guys there are there? They'll give up and go home without even thinking that Filip might not be there."

Arisha sat back with a grin. "Oh, that was perfect. Why can't all jobs be that much fun?"

QBS *ArchAngel*

Stephen, resting with one arm around Jennifer's shoulders and enjoying her small snores more than he would ever admit—was roused by ADAM at four.

"Emeric has just arrived in Madrid and has gotten a hotel room near the broadcasting station. There is one other figure in his hotel room. I believe it is Sidonie."

"I'll get everyone ready. Let me know as soon as they start moving in the morning."

"I will."

Stephen eased his arm out from under Jennifer's shoulders and tucked the blanket around her, then began to pace.

Storming the facilities had been difficult, the stuff of nightmares, but this job would be worse in a way. There was no way to guarantee that he could talk Emeric down, and if he could not talk him down...

He would need to kill him.

Stephen could not view that as anything but a failure. He had been sent here to fix this, and instead, he might end up killing one of the victims.

Where had he gone wrong?

Jennifer murmured and shifted in her sleep, and Stephen looked at her with a smile.

His smile faded as he considered something new. This whole time, he had tried to solve this the way he solved problems as Michael's liaison: by enforcing immutable rules and being the sole dispenser of justice.

But that wasn't what he needed to be any longer. When Bethany Anne left to go through the gate, there would no longer be the traditional hierarchy in the Unknown World.

What Stephen needed to do was help build a world that could stand on its own, without him.

Madrid, Spain

Emeric Carre did not sleep. He let Sidonie sleep in the big bed while he sat in a high-backed chair and watched the sky lighten.

He felt no anticipation, he realized. He did not even feel satisfaction.

He felt nothing.

It had been less than a week since he had freed himself from the hellhole of that laboratory; since he had torn the guards and scientists to shreds. All he felt was regret that his revenge had not taken more time.

Regret…and the growing fear that nothing would take away the void.

It was always with him, a pit of dark emptiness where he should have a soul. It stalked him, it rippled beneath his feet, it beckoned him down into it. When he remembered the months of pain, the forced transformations, all the things he had done at their command. It reached out to him with whispers, and he felt himself tilt downward toward it.

Rage was the only thing that drowned the whispers out. When he raged at all of them—the smug politicians and the lucky humans, the people who never once had to worry about being deconstructed in a laboratory—then, he was free of the void.

When his father asked him why he did not take a mate and have children, Emeric wanted to snarl that he would never do such a thing to anyone else. Why would he bear children who would be invisible and hunted their whole lives? He could not bear that. It would kill him, slowly but surely.

At least if he died tomorrow, it would be showing who he truly was.

And he would be free of the void, and the fear.

A knock sounded at the door, and he turned his head sharply. Sidonie had woken up, and she pushed herself up to answer the knock.

"*Non.*" Emeric motioned her back, to hide in the closet. "I will get it."

It could only be one thing, after all—danger.

When he peered through the peephole, it was to see only one figure, a man alone. He waited quietly.

Emeric opened the door, half expecting the vampire's claws to shoot out and pierce his throat.

But Stephen only inclined his head.

"May I speak with you?" he asked.

It was an honest question. Emeric narrowed his eyes, wondering what game this man could be playing. Driven by some urge he could not understand, he stood back to let the man enter.

Stephen was very aware of the Wechselbalg at his back as he walked into the room.

This was foolish. Going unarmed, alone, to meet with his enemy…was not wise.

The thought of the lecture he was going to get from Bethany Anne was almost enough to make him smile, though.

He turned to watch Emeric follow him into the room. The man's tall frame was held with the wary attention of someone completely exhausted. After what he had been through, Stephen could not blame him.

He knew better than to mention it.

"Why are you here?" Emeric asked, without preamble.

"Because in some ways, you were right." Stephen lifted his shoulders. "I enforced justice on your behalf without asking what justice you wanted."

"Doesn't that make me right in all ways?" Despite his combative words, Emeric did not look pleased.

"No." Stephen shook his head. "To know what I knew and do nothing would have been something I could never live with. We knew that the facilities had been going for some time and that no one had stopped them. We knew that various governments were turning a blind eye to what Hugo did. We couldn't rely on anyone else to stop him."

Emeric looked away.

"The politician you want to kill," Stephen said quietly. He marked how Emeric's head jerked around, and the hunted look in his eyes. "He's crooked as hell, isn't he? He knew what he was sheltering?"

"No." Emeric shook his head. "That's why it's worse, in a way. He didn't even care. A man said to him, 'I want you to look the other way from these facilities, I want you to tell the police not to investigate if they hear something,' and he just agreed without asking for any more details. We know it happened, we have the transcripts; his secretary ratted him out a few months ago to the Bureau of Internal Affairs." His face twisted. "But he's popular, so they didn't do anything, either.

"He just wanted the money so he could have fancy dinners, and in exchange, he told people not to help us! People who might have found us, saved us..." His voice broke, and he dropped his face into his hands.

It was jarring to see so big a man cry. Stephen swallowed, but he could not look away.

"They might have saved us," Emeric whispered again. "Children died in there. It should never have happened. There were investigations, and people like that man—like Fraga—they shut them down."

Stephen knew he could not speak too quickly, could not hammer a rhetorical point home, but he was compelled to speak. "Those were humans, weren't they, Emeric? The ones who tried to investigate?"

Emeric looked at him, his red-rimmed eyes haunted.

"How many others did this man kill by looking the other way?" Stephen continued. "How many human lives did he sacrifice? He didn't let you die because of what you were. He let you die along with everyone else because he doesn't care about anyone."

"They came for us because of what we were, though." Emeric shook his head. "I can't live in a world where my pack is hunted! I may not be an alpha, but I can't stand aside and let them be hurt, killed like animals! You have to understand that!"

"I do," Stephen said quietly.

That stopped Emeric in his tracks. "What?"

"I understand." Stephen lifted his shoulders. "Why do you think I liberated those facilities? I couldn't stand by and wait, knowing that I had the capabilities to storm them without a single person dying—a single innocent person, anyway. I understand what it is to not be able to sit by idly while innocent people suffer."

Emeric looked away.

"But I also know," Stephen said quietly. "What it is to act too rashly, to blame people who were not responsible for what they did. I am not saying that Julio Fraga is one of those," he clarified when Emeric's face darkened. "But I have learned over the years that justice is best dispensed coldly and quickly, with a clear mind. Vigilante justice… leads to the heart ruling the head. And when that happens, justice turns into a bloodbath, and the innocent are caught in the middle."

Emeric was silent. Behind him, Sidonie appeared. Her face was drawn and tired, and she was frowning. Stephen could see his words sinking into her heart as well.

Stephen continued. "If you want to be an alpha, you will have to learn what is truly in the best interests of a pack, and act according to that—not according to what would sate your thirst for revenge. That is the alpha's struggle.

"You might be an alpha one day, Emeric. You want to protect people. You want to let them live good, free lives. But not every urge we have in this world is good and just. Not every whim can be indulged without trampling on others—and the humans, the ones you resent so much, they are also a part of this world. They are clever and courageous...sometimes. They have every good and bad quality we have, save for the skills we have in battle.

"I don't know what type of world you will rule. The truth of the Unknown World may not stay hidden forever, and if it comes out, pack leaders will have to lead differently than they have before."

Emeric was silent for a long time. He walked past Stephen to the window and looked down on the streets. The first people were emerging from their apartments, mainly bankers hoping to get to the office before anyone else and capitalize on early information from the Asian markets. There were street sweepers and bus drivers carrying bagged lunches, and women opening up flower stands.

It was a world he had never been a part of...because he had never let himself be a part of it.

"What do you want from me?" he asked Stephen finally.

"I want you to be an alpha," Stephen said seriously. "I want you to think what would be best for the people you rescued—not what would slake their bloodlust, but what would be *best* for them. I want you to forge alliances with the other packs you helped make whole, the packs that were fractured by these facilities. And I want you to consider the fact that my brother, Michael, acted in concert with many governments, aiding them in work no one else could do. There is no reason you cannot be a part of this world, Emeric. But do so as the man you were meant to be, not a child."

When Emeric said nothing, Stephen smiled.

NATALIE GREY & MICHAEL ANDERLE

"And, if it helps...there might just be investigators waiting at that television station this morning to arrest Mr. Fraga. The world is going to find out just what he did."

Emeric looked at Sidonie. He saw the same twist of uncertainty and fear in her eyes that he recognized from his own.

He thought of home, with the sun rising over the fields in the summer. He could smell the wood smoke at the hearth in the winter and the smell of beef stew and fresh-baked bread. He could remember the youngest children laughing as they learned to transform into wolf cubs—and not wanting to turn back when they found out how much more agile they were as wolves.

The thought of home, of building a pack, seemed to make the void inside him fade.

He looked up at Stephen.

"What are you going to do?" Stephen asked.

"I'm going home," Emeric said. "I'm going home, and we're going to rebuild."

Stephen smiled.

EPILOGUE

"You're sure you want to do this?" Bethany Anne smiled at Jennifer.

Jennifer smiled. "I am."

"Because you still have a year left on your contract."

"I'm sure," Jennifer said, laughing.

"And you've talked to your parents about this?" Bethany Anne asked. Her eyes widened when she saw the shifty look in Jennifer's eyes. "You haven't!"

"Better to ask forgiveness than permission," Jennifer said, with great dignity. She pointed to the paper. "Now, come on. I want to sign."

Bethany Anne stepped back, sweeping her hand out at the paper.

Jennifer signed with a flourish, no hesitation in her as she wrote her name.

This was it. No more uncertainty. No more, "when my contract is up," no more wondering. Her place was here, with TQB. In the past years, she had seen more of the world, and done more to be proud of, than she had in her whole life before that. Now she would be a protector for those she loved most.

She stared down at the paper for a moment and then stepped back. "Done."

"Welcome aboard." Bethany Anne grinned.

Pete clapped her on the shoulder and Nathan gave her a nod from the other side of the room. Ashur even came to stick his cold nose into her hand, making her jump. *Full-time members of TQB have to pet me,* his manner said clearly.

Jennifer laughed and obeyed, crouching and scratching her nails over the fur around his neck. Ashur let his eyes drift closed and wagged his tail.

Stephen slipped into the room and looked around at everyone's faces. His eyes flicked to Bethany Anne's. "What did I miss? Why am I here?"

"Oh, it's no big deal." Bethany Anne smiled and jerked her head at Pete and Nathan. "Just some news from Jennifer. Come on, Ashur. Let's go."

Ashur grumbled but plodded after the group.

Jennifer stood. She was so nervous her palms were clammy. She hadn't told Stephen she was doing this. What if he thought she was clingy? What if he thought it was a terrible idea, and this had all just been a fling for him?

"I, uh..." Suddenly she could not remember a single word of English.

Stephen strolled closer. He could see a blush rising in Jennifer's cheeks, fear and hope all tumbled together in her eyes.

Then he saw the piece of paper.

His heart stopped, and in a single, dizzying moment, he admitted to himself that he had been afraid.

Afraid she would leave.

"You're staying?" He could not keep the hope out his voice.

"Yeah." Jennifer's voice came out high, and she twisted her hands. "Yes. I...hope that's—"

Stephen swept her into his arms with a grin and stared down at her.

"It is exactly what I want," he told her.

"Hey!" Pete barged his way into the room and groaned when he saw Jennifer and Stephen. He covered his eyes with one hand and turned his head away purposefully. "*Ahem.* There's something you two should see."

"We're...kind of having a moment." Jennifer tried to keep the annoyance out of her voice.

"No, really. You're gonna want to see this." Pete nodded seriously. "Bobcat. Just gave up testing a beer. To go out with a *girl.*"

Jennifer and Stephen both darted out of the room in time to see Bobcat leaving with a dark-haired woman, while a giant dog trailed at their heels. Beer lay abandoned on a table nearby.

Stephen gave a low whistle.

"So...when's the wedding?"

"We're taking bets now," Bethany Anne informed him. She leaned over to look at Jennifer. "And now that you're part of the permanent crew, you get to bet too!"

FINIS

AUTHOR NOTES - NATALIE GREY

WRITTEN JULY 17, 2018

Thank you all for your patience as you waited for the conclusion of Trials & Tribulations! Stephen & Jennifer are an amazing couple, truly bringing out the best in each other. Both of them have such a strong sense of duty, and yet they're incredibly determined to stand on their own and not rely on anyone - which is infuriating for both of them! (And well deserved. Also that.)

A huge thank you, as always, to Michael - you invited me into this world and I'm so grateful. I've met some of my favorite characters here, as well as some truly amazing (real-life) people!

Another thank you to my readers. I can't wait to share more stories from the Kurtherian Gambit and the other series already begun and yet to come! I am so lucky to be able to do what I do for a living.

Finally, thank you to B and L, who fill my life with joy every day.

-Nat

AUTHOR NOTES - MICHAEL ANDERLE

JULY 17, 2018

First, THANK YOU for taking your time to read our stories, and read all the way to the back with these *Author Notes*.

I have to admit something…

We lost this book.

You see, it was finished a LONG time ago, and we had it on our schedule to publish, then <redacted> happened and we lost track…

Our publishing schedule is fast and furious, and we had a few hiccups, and then it got dark a few times, and we slept.

That was probably our big mistake.

Finally, with Natalie working on the Barnabas books, (and a fan hitting me up on Facebook asking about this book) we started looking. I even went back to Natalie and asked and sonofabitch if even she wasn't scratching her head for a little while. Eventually (obviously) we found the book and got it on the docket for publishing... Then we realized WE HAD NO COVER.

H#ly @#%@.

It's like this book was fighting us, being the little black sheep that didn't want to go out on stage or something. However, like two parents, Natalie and I did what we needed to do.

We shoved it out (like a mama bird) and told it to FLY!

So, cover so new you can smell the digital paint and all, I hope you enjoyed this book!

Ad Aeternitatem,

Michael Anderle

BOOKS BY NATALIE GREY

Shadows of Magic

Bound Sorcery

Blood Sorcery

Bright Sorcery

Set in the Kurtherian Gambit Universe

Bellatrix

Challenges

Risk Be Damned

Damned to Hell

To Hell and Back

The Vigilante Chronicles

Vigilante (1) Sentinel (2) - Warden (3)

Writing as Moira Katson

Shadowborn

Shadowforged

Shadow's End

Daughter of Ashes

Mahalia

BOOKS BY MICHAEL ANDERLE

For a complete list of books by Michael Anderle, please visit:

www.lmbpn.com/ma-books/

All LMBPN Audiobooks are Available at Audible.com and
iTunes. For a complete list of audiobooks visit:

www.lmbpn.com/audible

Facebook Here:
https://www.facebook.com/TheKurtherianGambitBooks/

www.ingramcontent.com/pod-product-compliance
Lightning Source LLC
Chambersburg PA
CBHW050257110726
47898CB00007B/2451